D0425154

Genie With the Light Blue Hair

Other Bantam Starfire Books by Ellen Conford

Hail, Hail Camp Timberwood
Anything for a Friend
The Things I Did for Love

Genie With the Light Blue Hair

Ellen Conford

BANTAM BOOKS
TORONTO · NEW YORK · LONDON · SYDNEY · AUCKLAND

GENIE WITH THE LIGHT BLUE HAIR
A Bantam Book / March 1989

The Starfire logo is a registered trademark of Bantam Books, a division of Bantam Doubleday Dell Publishing Group, Inc. Registered in U.S. Patent and Trademark Office and elsewhere.

All rights reserved.
Copyright © 1989 by Conford Enterprises, Ltd.
Book design by Anne Ling.
No part of this book may be reproduced or transmitted in any form or by any means, electronic or mechanical, including photocopying, recording, or by any information storage and retrieval system, without permission in writing from the publisher.
For information address: Bantam Books.

Library of Congress Cataloging-in-Publication Data

Conford, Ellen.
   Genie with the light blue hair / Ellen Conford.
      p.   cm.
   Summary: When Jean finds a wish-granting genie in the lamp she receives for her birthday, she discovers that having all her wishes come true isn't as wonderful as she thinks it will be.
   ISBN 0-553-05806-1
   [1. Wishes—Fiction.   2. Self-respect—Fiction.]   I. Title.
PZ7.C7593Ge   1989
[Fic]—dc19   88-7777
                                                                  CIP
                                                                  AC

Published simultaneously in the United States and Canada

Bantam Books are published by Bantam Books, a division of Bantam Doubleday Dell Publishing Group, Inc. Its trademark, consisting of the words "Bantam Books" and the portrayal of a rooster, is Registered in U.S. Patent and Trademark Office and in other countries. Marca Registrada. Bantam Books, 666 Fifth Avenue, New York, New York 10103.

PRINTED IN THE UNITED STATES OF AMERICA

FG   0 9 8 7 6 5 4 3 2 1

Genie With the Light Blue Hair

One

The first fourteen years of my life were fairly un-eventful, but on my fifteenth birthday something rather unusual happened.

The day started out no differently from any of my other birthdays. My parents gave me practical gifts, which were just what I wanted: an unabridged dictionary, a gold-plated pen with my initials engraved on it, and *The Complete Guide to Movies on TV*.

My ten-year-old brother, Richie, gave me a wallet—which, even though it wasn't leather, certainly was not bought with his own money.

Then we went out for breakfast at The Hotcake House, where the waitress served me a plate of pancakes with a candle stuck in the middle, and everyone sang "Happy Birthday."

Richie, of course, sang, "Happy birthday to you, you belong in a zoo, you look like a monkey and you act like one too."

It was embarrassing but predictable. My parents are reasonable people, but birthdays bring out the worst in them.

Since May 1 fell on a Sunday this year, my Uncle Rocky and Aunt Jean were coming for a "gala birthday dinner" in the late afternoon.

Aunt Jean is my mother's sister and my godmother. I was named for her. She fusses over me even more than my own mother does. Maybe it's because she doesn't have any children of her own to fuss over. I don't know.

I would have been just as happy to spend the day reading in my room and eating sandwiches. I don't think there's anything that great about birthdays.

My aunt and uncle arrived at four o'clock. At 4:01 Uncle Rocky said, "Didn't you invite any of your little friends to your birthday party?"

"I'm fifteen," I said. "I don't have any little friends."

"She doesn't have any big ones, either," Richie said.

"I do too, you vile toad."

"Don't be so touchy, Jeannie," my mother said. "We all just want you to have a happy birthday."

"Not all of us," Richie said.

"Open your present," said Aunt Jean. Uncle Rocky put a large, square package on the coffee table. It was wrapped in blue-and-gold paper and tied with a gold ribbon.

"I hope you like it," Aunt Jean said. "We didn't want to get you a book again, and I wasn't sure what else you'd like."

"Another book would have been fine with me." My father scowled at me.

"But I'm sure I'll like this," I added. "The wrapping is beautiful." I didn't want to hurt their feelings.

"It's something practical," said Uncle Rocky. I pulled the paper off the box. "We know you like practical presents."

The box was white. "Unique Antiques" was printed on the top. I couldn't imagine what kind of antique they thought would be practical.

I opened the box and took out my present. I still couldn't imagine what kind of antique it was.

It looked like a silver gravy server, but bigger. It was the size and shape of a teapot.

Maybe it *was* a teapot. Why Aunt Jean thought I wanted a teapot was beyond me, but I tried to smile appreciatively.

I took the lid off. Inside was a fat blue candle.

So it was a candleholder in the shape of a teapot.

"Gee," I said. "A candleholder in the shape of a teapot. It's just what I always wanted."

My father and mother both glared at me. I guess I didn't sound very enthusiastic.

"Jean, is that real silver?" my mother asked.

"No, just silver plate."

"But even silver plate—"

"It really wasn't that expensive," Aunt Jean said.

I could believe it. Who knows how long that thing would have stayed at Unique Antiques if my aunt hadn't come along?

"They couldn't even verify that it's an antique," Aunt Jean said.

"You know what it looks like?" Richie said. "Aladdin's magic lamp."

"I thought so too," said Uncle Rocky. "But we rubbed it and nothing happened. Maybe the genie will come out for Jeannie. Hey! A genie for Jeannie. That's funny!"

"A genie for Jeannie," I said. "Cute." Why couldn't they have given me a book?

"Let me rub it," said Richie. I handed him the lamp.

"We thought this would be a good emergency light for your room," said Aunt Jean. "Especially during the summer, when there are so many thunderstorms."

"For when the electricity goes out," added Uncle Rocky.

"Sure, right," I said. "Like a flashlight."

"But with this you don't have to worry about batteries," he said.

The electricity almost never fails on our street because the power lines are underground. The only time the lights blow out is when my mother and I both turn on our hair dryers at the same time.

"This doesn't work," said Richie. "It's not magic at all."

He handed me the lamp. I didn't think it would work even as a lamp. The candle was shorter than the kettle. How could it give off any light if the flame was below the rim of the kettle?

And why a lid? If you put the lid on, you wouldn't see the candle at all, and without any air it would go right out.

Uncle Rocky shook his head. "Maybe it wasn't such a good idea."

4

"No, it's a fine idea," I said. "It's just what I need. Thank you. Besides, it's the thought that counts."

"I knew she wouldn't like it," he muttered.

My parents glared at me.

"I like it, I like it!" I clutched the lamp against my chest. "I wouldn't trade it for anything." I'd sell it for a dime, I thought.

"Let's eat," my mother said. "We've made all of Jeannie's favorites. Shrimp cocktail—"

"Yicchh," said Richie.

"Japanese miso soup—"

"Blecchh," said Richie.

"And roast duck à l'orange."

"Quack," said Richie.

It wasn't a bad birthday as birthdays go. After dinner Uncle Rocky took me aside and slipped a ten-dollar bill into my hand. "Buy something you really like," he whispered.

Just before they left, Aunt Jean cornered me in the kitchen and tucked a twenty-dollar bill into my skirt pocket.

"I meant to put it inside the lamp, but I forgot," she said.

And then, after they left, we all watched one of my favorite movies on the VCR: *A Night at the Opera*. The Marx Brothers always make me laugh, no matter how down I am.

I had a last piece of birthday cheesecake and went up to my room.

"Close your windows," my mother said. "It's just starting to rain."

I heard a clap of thunder in the distance. "It's so hot up here," I complained. My room is on the third floor, in what used to be the attic. It's cold in the winter and hot in the summer, but it's private.

"Close them until the storm is over," she said. "It should cool off after the rain."

I put Aunt Jean's present on my night table and shut the windows. I have a small fan on my desk but it doesn't do much except blow the hot air around.

I wasn't sleepy yet, so I sat down at my desk and opened the new dictionary. I closed my eyes, and with my new pen, made a circle in the air over the page. Then I brought the pen down till it touched the page.

I opened my eyes and looked at the word the pen had landed on. "Man."

Boring. I already knew that word.

I've played this game since I was a kid. I pick out words at random and make a list of them. Sometimes I use them to tell my fortune. Sometimes I try to make up a little story including all the words on the list.

And sometimes I just learn some really weird words.

I flipped the pages and picked another word. I opened my eyes. "Snuggle." Hmmm. Man and snuggle. I immediately thought of Mr. Kellogg, my English teacher—the man I would most like to snuggle with. But I don't indulge in impossible dreams.

I riffled through the pages of the dictionary one more time, closed my eyes, and circled my pen over the words.

Suddenly there was a tremendous clap of thunder and a bolt of lightning so bright that I could see it even through my closed eyelids.

"YIKES!" I opened my eyes. It was completely dark in my room. I blinked a couple of times, trying to see.

"Jeannie?" my father called. "Are you okay?"

"It's dark in here!"

"The lights went out. That was a close one."

Another flash of lightning lit up my room for a moment. I noticed the teapot lamp on my night table.

"Hey!" I yelled. "If someone would bring me a match I could light this stupid lamp Aunt Jean gave me. I don't think it will do any good, but . . ."

"Coming right up." A flashlight beam shone on the stairway, and my mother came into my room.

"Are you going to be all right up here?" she asked. She handed me a book of matches.

"Of course," I said. "I'm not afraid. A thunderstorm is a natural phenomenon."

"I used to tell you it was God bowling," she said.

"That's all right," I said. "I never believed you."

She trained the beam of the flashlight on the lamp.

"Isn't it funny," she said, "that we have a storm the day Aunt Jean gives you the lamp?"

I shrugged. "Just a coincidence."

"But what about losing the electricity? You know how unusual that is."

"It's happened before," I said. "But it will be a good thing to say in a thank-you note."

I took the lid off and struck a match. I had to reach

down into the lamp because the candle was so short and stubby. I nearly burned my fingertips before the wick caught the flame.

"Ow!" I shook the match out and dropped it inside the pot.

I was surprised to see how brightly the candle burned. Even though it was way down inside the lamp, the flame on the wick grew until it looked longer than the candlestick.

"How about that?" my mother said. "It gives off a lot of light."

"You didn't think it would work either, did you?" I smiled.

My mother looked around the room. The candlelight was casting flickering shadows on the walls and the sloping attic ceiling.

"It's a little spooky," she said.

"I guess if you have an overactive imagination . . ." I let my voice trail off. Actually, I thought the shadows were kind of interesting. I couldn't remember ever seeing my room by candlelight before.

"You won't be nervous about being alone?" she said.

"What's there to be nervous about? They're just shadows."

"Good thing you're not troubled by an overactive imagination," my mother said dryly.

"I'm fifteen years old," I said. "And I was never afraid of the dark anyway."

"I know." She grinned and kissed me. "Happy birthday again."

She closed the door as she left my room. I sat down

on the bed. There wasn't enough light to read by, but I could see plainly enough to get undressed.

I kicked off a shoe. The light grew a little brighter. I looked at the lamp. The flame seemed higher than it had been a moment ago.

No. Candles burn down, not up. It must be an optical illusion.

I took off my other shoe. I tossed it into my closet.

The flame of the candle was now higher than the top of the pot.

"This is impossible," I said to myself. "I must be imagining things."

But I never imagine things. I mean, nothing weird. As my mother said, I don't have an overactive imagination. Even when I was little I never believed in Santa Claus.

As I stared at the lamp from across the room, I saw a little wisp of smoke rise up from the flame. The smoke seemed to be blue. Another puff of smoke followed. They floated toward the ceiling. The second puff joined the first one, and formed what looked like a chubby, upside-down exclamation point.

"There's a rational explanation for this," I told myself. "It must be air currents, or some unusual atmospheric disturbance."

There was nothing to be afraid of. I was on my way to bed anyway. I'd just blow out the candle.

Somehow I didn't feel as sure of myself as I was trying to convince myself I was. I didn't even want to move toward the bed, let alone get in it. The lamp was on the night table right next to it.

My room got brighter and yet more shadowy at the same time. The lamp seemed to light up certain areas very strongly, but outside the glow of the candlelight, in the shadowy corners of my room, everything was in deepest darkness.

I'm being silly, I told myself. All I have to do is put out the candle and there won't be any more shadows.

I took a step toward my bed.

The upside-down exclamation point was growing. Larger. Larger. Until it was the size of an adult human.

It hovered halfway between the floor and the ceiling. If I opened my window and turned on the fan, maybe I could blow it away.

But the fan wouldn't work without electricity, and my legs didn't seem to support me very well, so I didn't think I'd make it to the window.

Not that there was anything to be afraid of.

I wanted to shut my eyes and wait till it went away—whatever it was—but that would be childish. I stared intently at the smoke. As I looked at it, I began to see a body.

I gasped. The body was blue. It had on long, billowy harem pants. And a blue vest. It was entirely blue, from the top of its turban to the tips of its pointy-slippered feet.

Now I began to see a face. It was blue also, except for a thick black moustache that looked as if it had been painted on with shoe polish, and bushy black eyebrows. It wore a pair of black-framed eyeglasses.

I could see arms. And hands, and fingers. It was holding a long, black cigar between its thumb and forefinger.

"Help," I squeaked. "Help."

But the words stuck in my throat. I was weak with fright.

The shadow tapped the cigar with its middle finger.

"Got a light?"

Two

"What—how—who—"

I couldn't finish a sentence. I couldn't talk at all. I moved backward till I was inside my closet. I wanted to climb into the laundry hamper, where I used to hide when I was five.

Unfortunately, I haven't been able to fit in the hamper since I was five. So I clutched a dress hanging next to me and tried to hide behind it.

It wasn't hot in my room anymore. I was shivering.

"Oh, good," the smoke said. It bent down and stuck its cigar into the lamp. It puffed a few times, then exhaled a long, thin stream of blue smoke.

I finally found my voice. "I hate cigar smoke."

"So don't smoke cigars," he replied.

"I meant, your cigar smoke."

He blew out a puff of smoke right toward me. "Don't be such a killjoy. You can't even smell it."

It was true. I sniffed as the smoke wafted by the closet. I couldn't smell a thing.

13

"I wish you'd leave anyway," I said, my voice still squeaky. "I don't know how you got in here, or why you're wearing that costume, but—"

There was something familiar about his face. Even though it was blue, I felt I'd seen it somewhere before.

"But you called me," he said.

"I what?"

"You called me."

"I did not." I was completely mystified. "I don't even know *what* to call you."

"Arthur," he said.

"Arthur?"

"And you lit the lamp, so here I am. What do you want?"

I was getting dizzy. "What do you mean, what do I want?"

"Why do you repeat everything I say?" he asked.

"This is ridiculous," I said. I stepped out of the closet. But I stayed right in front of it, just in case. "I know what happened. I was somehow knocked out by that bolt of lightning and this is all a dream. Like *The Wizard of Oz*."

Arthur took another puff of his cigar and a stream of blue smoke rings curled toward the ceiling. He eyed them, his head cocked to one side.

Suddenly I realized who he looked like.

Groucho Marx.

"This *is* ridiculous," I said. "Now I know I'm dreaming."

"You repeat everything you say too," he commented. "But it's okey dokey with me. I'm just glad to be out of that lamp." He tilted his head toward the night table.

14

"You mean—"

He nodded. "It gets boring in there. So, what can I do for you? Money, fame, power, love?"

"Wait a minute, wait a minute." I walked slowly toward the night table. Even though I have no imagination, I felt I must have conjured this thing up myself. My mother had inspired it with the suggestion that the shadows were spooky.

I was probably just seeing silhouettes on the wall, and as soon as the lights came back on, this apparition would disappear.

"You seem a little slow," the apparition said. "Most people can tell right away that I'm a genie. The lamp, the turban—it's kind of classic."

"A genie?"

"There you go again." But he smiled. I think. On a blue-smoke face it's hard to tell. His moustache moved.

"You can't be a genie," I said firmly. "There is no such thing. Genies are only in fairy tales. Besides, whoever heard of a genie who looks like Groucho Marx?"

"You've got it backward," he said. "Groucho Marx looked like me. I've had this face longer than he ever did."

"All right," I said. "Fun's fun. But how did you get in my room and what do you want?"

"You called me," he said impatiently. "You lit the lamp, I came out. What's so hard to understand?"

"Okay," I said to myself. "This is a dream. Maybe this is some sort of imagination breakdown. All the years that I've been sensible and rational could have resulted in a

15

drastic strain on my brain, and this fantasy is my mind's way of telling me it needs a rest."

And since the last thing I saw tonight was a Marx Brothers movie, why not dream up a genie who looks like Groucho Marx?

Fine. I'll play along. As long as I remember that he's only a phantom of my own creation, everything will be under control.

I really felt much calmer now. I walked to my desk and perched on top of it. I could see his face more clearly here.

"All right," I said. "So what now? Do I get three wishes?"

"Is that all you want?" he asked.

"You mean I can have more than three? How many wishes do I get?"

"It depends," he said. "There's no specific number."

"What does it depend on?"

"I can't tell you that," he said.

"Oh, fine. I get anywhere from three to a million wishes but you won't tell me when I'll run out of wishes."

"I don't know myself," he said. "It's different with everybody. Say, how's Marilyn Monroe looking?"

"Marilyn Monroe?"

"*Again* with the repeating?" He raised his eyebrows.

"She's dead," I said.

He sighed. "Too bad. She was quite attractive—in a fleshy sort of way." He let out two long streams of smoke They formed the shape of an hourglass.

"How long ago?" he asked. "What year is this?"

16

"1988," I told him.

"That's not too bad. I've only been in for thirty-three years. Look, it's not that I don't enjoy chatting with you, but you really have to find something for me to do. Isn't there *anything* you want?"

"Sure," I answered. "Lots of things, but not the kind of things you mean. I don't want money or power." Love sounded good, though.

"I am not getting through to you," he said. "Try and concentrate." He spoke very slowly and distinctly. "I am your genie. I am in your power. You make a wish and I make it come true. Now, would you please wish for something?"

"All right, all right," I said. "Let's clear up this non-sense once and for all. I wish I had a boyfriend."

"Okey dokey."

!

Before I could blink there was a boy standing next to my desk. He was blond, several inches taller than me, and very handsome. He was holding a bouquet of roses.

I screamed.

"I love you," he said.

"Get him out of here!" I cried.

The boy disappeared. "Make up your mind," Arthur said. "Do you realize that if you only had three wishes you'd have used up two of them already?"

"You do not exist." I tried to stay calm. "I am going to bed now. When I wake up you will be gone."

17

"I hate to tell you this, but if you want to get rid of me all you have to do is blow out the candle."

"Just blow out the candle?"

"This echo is getting tiresome," he said. "I'd just as soon go back in the lamp for a couple of decades till someone interesting calls me."

I was beginning to wonder if I had a strong enough imagination to dream up this whole scene. Maybe I hadn't imagined it. Maybe that blond boy was real. He certainly looked real.

But if that were true, then the universe had no rules. Everything we'd always been taught about physics and space and weather and cause and effect—it was all wrong.

If Arthur was really a genie who could grant me any wish I asked for, I could control the world.

Or turn the earth upside down.

Or buy France.

Or go to the moon.

The possibilities were incredible.

And all I'd asked for was a boyfriend!

"I'm beginning to believe you, I think. But tell me how you got that boy into my room."

"You wish and I deliver."

"But was he real?" I asked. "I mean, did you create him or did you transport him from somewhere else?"

"This is technical stuff," Arthur said. "Too complicated. You don't want to bother your head about it."

"Hey, it's not the 1950's anymore," I said. "Women can understand anything men can."

"But humans can't understand everything genies can," he said.

"Good point," I admitted. "All right, if you're really a genie tell me what tomorrow's *New York Times* headline will be."

"I'm a genie, not a fortune-teller." He sounded bored. "Fortune-telling is a whole different skill, and it has nothing to do with granting wishes."

He hovered over the lamp as if he were impatient to go back inside. "Why don't you blow out the candle and forget all about this and I'll come back in a century or so to help somebody who really needs me."

"No!" I said. I was surprised at how emotional I sounded. "There are only two possible explanations for you. Either you're a real genie or I'm hallucinating. If you're real, I have plenty of things to ask you for. And if I'm hallucinating, I'll think I'm getting them."

"Very logical," he said.

"I try to be," I replied. "Now, I don't want to waste wishes on stupid things." I remembered the story about the woman who got three wishes and blew all three of them by wishing that her husband had a pudding on his nose.

"So what I'm going to do," I said, "is make a list."

"That sounds sensible," he said. "Most people start wishing for the first thing that pops into their heads. Usually money."

"Well, I know that money can't buy happiness."

"You'd be surprised," said Arthur, "at how much happiness money can buy."

"Whatever," I said. "I'm going to send you back into the lamp now and start working on my list. I'll see you tomorrow."

"Okey dokey."

I blew out the candle. At least, I tried to. It flickered and flared up as Arthur began to whirl around faster and faster, like a blue cyclone.

Finally the candle went out and all of Arthur's blue smoke disappeared inside the lamp.

I put the lid back on.

Without the light from the lamp, my room was pitch dark. The electricity hadn't been restored yet, so I couldn't start working on my wish list.

I began to feel how hot and sticky it still was in my room. While I was talking to Arthur I'd been much too involved to think about the weather, but as I took off my clothes they were damp with perspiration.

I reached into my dresser and groped around till I felt a cotton nightshirt. I slipped it over my head. It wasn't raining anymore, so I went over to the window and opened it.

I leaned out the window to take a deep breath of fresh, rain-cooled air. But it was even more humid outside than in my room, and I felt as if I were breathing into a wet sweat sock.

An air conditioner, I thought. I wish I had an air conditioner up here. Though it wouldn't be any use without electricity.

Arthur! I could get an air conditioner. All I had to do was ask Arthur for one. If he was real he'd bring me an air conditioner. If he wasn't, I was a mental case, which would be a lot more serious than feeling a little warm.

I fumbled around my night table for the matches. I

took the lid of the lamp off and struck a match. Again I had some trouble reaching the wick, but I got it lit.

Sure enough, two puffs of blue smoke rose from the lamp and joined to form the upside-down exclamation point I had seen before.

The features became clear once more, but the cigar was missing.

"You called?" he said.

"Yes. It's awfully hot in here. I'll never be able to sleep. I wish it were cooler."

"Okey dokey," said Arthur.

!

Before he finished saying "dokey" I was knee-deep in snow. Snow showered down on me from the ceiling. Gusts of wind whipped around the furniture, nearly tearing off my nightshirt. Six inches of slush covered my bed.

"This isn't what I meant!"

"You don't want snow?" Arthur asked.

"NO!"

"Okey dokey."

!

The snow vanished instantly. My room was a tropical forest again.

"Then what do you want?" he said.

"An air conditioner," I said. "And the electricity to

make it go," I added. I didn't want to get stuck on a technicality again.

"Why didn't you say so in the first place?" he asked.

!

An air conditioner appeared in my window. It was humming softly. A cool draft washed over me. It felt wonderful.

"You're going to have to be more specific," Arthur grumbled. "I'm not a mind reader, you know."

"I'll make a list," I said, "of all the things I want, in order of importance."

"Good idea," said Arthur. "Call me when you're ready."

"Tomorrow," I said.

"Okey dokey," said Arthur.

Three

I woke up Monday morning sure that everything that happened after the lights went out last night was a dream. I pride myself on being a sensible, skeptical person. Ever since I discovered that the Tooth Fairy was my father, I have been very suspicious about the supernatural. I don't even read my horoscope in the newspaper.

I'd barely opened my eyes when Richie barged into my room. "Dad says do you want an Egg McMuffin?"

"Don't you knock?"

He knocked on the inside of my door. "Knock knock. Do you want an Egg McMuffin?"

"Yes," I said—and suddenly found that I was holding one in my hands.

Richie stared at me. Then he noticed the window. "Where did *that* come from?"

I didn't know if he meant the Egg McMuffin or the air conditioner that bulked out of the bottom half of my window.

I quickly stuffed the muffin under my pillow. It would be one less thing to explain.

"When did you get an air conditioner?" he asked.

"That's not an air conditioner," I said. "Go down and tell Dad that I want an Egg McMuffin."

"But you already—" He stared at me. He banged the side of his head with his hand. "Whoo-ee-oo. The Twilight Zone. You were just holding an Egg McMuffin."

"No I wasn't," I lied. "It was your imagination. Now get out of here so I can get dressed."

He pointed at the window. "And that isn't an air conditioner?"

"No," I said.

"One of us is crazy," he said.

"It's you."

He backed out of my room, gawking at me.

It was all real!

I still had the air conditioner, an Egg McMuffin had materialized out of nowhere, and it wasn't a figment of my imagination, because Richie saw those things too.

I heard footsteps on the stairs. I leaped out of bed and ran to light the lamp.

There was a knock on my door just as Arthur floated out of the lamp.

"You called?" he asked.

"Jeannie, open the door." My father.

"Get rid of the air conditioner!" I whispered.

"Okey dokey," said Arthur.

!

24

Poof—no air conditioner. I reached under my pillow for the McMuffin and tossed it out the window.

"Back in the lamp," I whispered to Arthur. I blew out the candle.

"Come in," I called.

My father and Richie came into my room.

"It's not there!" Richie yelled. "It was there a minute ago!"

"Rich, please," my father said. "I hate jokes on Monday mornings."

"But—"

"I'm going to get the Egg McMuffins now," my father said. "At this rate, no one will be out of here on time."

"But she just *had* an Egg McMuffin!" Richie insisted.

"Enough!" my father snapped. "You'd better start getting dressed, Jeannie. You'll be late for school."

"That would be no tragedy," I said.

Arthur was real! I actually had my own genie. I could have anything I wanted. All I had to do was ask.

I lit the blue candle again. "I wish I didn't have to go to school today."

!

I'd barely finished the sentence before I found myself flat on my back in bed, with my nose stuffed, my throat sore, and my head feeling as if it was on fire.

My mother was standing over me shaking a thermometer.

25

"No school for you today," she said.

"Wait a minute!" I croaked. "I don't want to be sick."

!

In the time I took to say it, I was back on my feet in the center of my room, temperature normal, throat feeling fine.

I shook my head. This genie stuff was pretty tricky. Obviously I didn't have the hang of it yet.

The problem with school was, I wasn't learning anything useful. The only challenge I faced as a high-school freshman was finding my classrooms before the late bell rang.

The school, Hungerford High, was enormous. Three junior high schools sent their graduates there, and every day I thought I would drown in a sea of unfamiliar faces.

I was never what you would call popular in junior high or elementary school, but at least there were people who said "Hi" to me in the halls.

Here at Hungerford I hardly knew anybody in any of my classes. To me everyone looked older and cooler and better dressed. They all seemed to know where they were going.

All I got out of high school was homework. And that was as boring as most of my teachers.

My parents said it was always tough being in the youngest class in any school, and they were sure I'd be happier as a sophomore.

I didn't believe them. Next year the school would still be huge and I would still be me, and I probably wouldn't have any more friends than I did now.

If only they taught social skills in high school. When it comes to socializing, I'm a moron.

I'm shy, but it's not only that. When I do say something, I say what I'm thinking. I don't know any other way to be. My mother always talks about telling "little white lies" to spare a person's feelings.

Like when I told Aunt Jean I liked the lamp.

But I find it hard to talk to people at all, and when I do I can't pretend to feel something I don't feel. I don't like being a hypocrite.

My mother says it's not being a hypocrite, it's being sensitive to other people's needs.

"People will like you," she always says, "if you show them that you like them."

If I have to pretend to like somebody, why would I want them to like me? It didn't make any sense. Besides, I couldn't pretend to like anyone at Hungerford High. I didn't know anyone.

Except for Lynn Shoemaker. If it weren't for Lynn, I don't know what I would do. She's been my friend since the sixth grade, and she really understands me.

I can tell her anything that's on my mind, and she still likes me. Even though she has other friends, she likes to be with me.

Now, the day after my birthday, I was dying to tell Lynn about my genie. It seemed to me that Arthur was the most incredible thing since the atom bomb, and I was bursting to tell someone about him.

27

But I wasn't sure I should. Ordinarily Lynn wouldn't tell anybody one of my secrets, but this secret wasn't ordinary.

I got through my morning classes by working on my wish list. If this day ever ended, I would go home and start wishing.

One of my wishes would be to never have a day like this again.

At lunch I met Lynn in the cafeteria. We'd walked to school together, and all she could talk about was the dance club. She was still talking about it.

"Tiffany Tupperman asked us to eat with her, okay?" she greeted me.

"She asked *us* or she asked *you*?" I said. "And can there really be a human being named Tiffany Tupperman?"

"I was talking to her in gym about the modern-dance club. She's the president. She said she'd tell me all about the club at lunch."

"It sounds simply thrilling." I couldn't tell Lynn my *really* thrilling news with Tiffany around, but it was just as well. It might be better to check with Arthur before telling Lynn about him.

It's hard to believe, but there *is* a human being named Tiffany Tupperman. She's one of those people in Hungerford who are older and slicker and better dressed than I would ever be.

She is tall and has a mass of dark, wavy hair that she pulls back with combs.

Today she was wearing a short denim skirt, a big red T-shirt, red tights and purple socks. I would have looked like something out of a thrift shop in that outfit.

28

She looked like a million dollars. And she had an extremely cute boyfriend named Ned Bayer.

Tiffany and Lynn started talking ballet. At first I felt pretty annoyed with Lynn for letting Tiffany eat with us. They were so involved in their discussion that I might as well not have been there.

I wondered why some people are the Tiffany Tuppermans of the world, and others are the Jean Warrens.

When the bell rang Lynn said, "I didn't realize we were talking so long. I'm sorry, Jeannie. We sort of ignored you, didn't we?"

"What do you mean, sort of?" I said.

"You ought to join the dance club, Lynn." Tiffany picked up her books. "You'd really enjoy it."

"I think I will," Lynn said. "At least I'll try it out. Do you want to come too, Jeannie?"

"I don't dance," I said. "Don't ask me."

Tiffany waggled her fingers at Lynn and walked off with just enough sway in her almost nonexistent hips to attract the attention of every male she passed.

Lynn shook her head. "Isn't she something? I really admire her."

"You're just as pretty as she is," I said.

"Thanks, but I don't think so. And it's not just how she looks. You know what I mean. She's kind of sophisticated and cool. If I could be any person I wanted to be, I'd want to be her."

I did know what she meant. I hated to admit it, because I try to be sensible and realistic, but the truth is, if I had to spend the next three years in Hungerford High,

I'd rather spend them as Tiffany Tupperman than as Jean Warren.

"You're terrific just the way you are," I told Lynn as we headed for the stairs. "I, on the other hand . . ."

Suddenly it hit me.

I, on the other hand, could be Tiffany Tupperman anytime I wanted to.

Four

When I got home at three o'clock that afternoon, I dashed up to my room without even taking off my jacket.

My parents both work and Richie doesn't come home till three-thirty so I had about half an hour to turn into Tiffany Tupperman.

I was sure that being Tiffany would solve all my problems. She was everything I wanted to be but wasn't. By the last period that afternoon. I was so excited by the thought of my transformation that my heart didn't even skip a beat when Mr. Kellogg called on me in English.

As Tiffany Tupperman I'd have it all. Looks, popularity, clothes, money, sophistication, cool, and an extremely handsome boyfriend named Ned Bayer.

I didn't plan to be Tiffany Tupperman permanently, but for a while I'd have a taste of the good life.

I took the lid off the lamp and lit the candle. I could hear my heart pounding as Arthur emerged from the lamp.

"Your wish is my command," he said. He flicked a cigar ash into the lamp.

"Can you turn me into somebody else?" I asked.

"That depends."

"Just tell me, before I make the wish, if it's possible for me to become someone else."

Arthur looked thoughtful. "Is this a person who's already alive, or do you want to be a whole new person?"

"This is a girl I know," I said. "I want to see how it feels to be her for a while."

"Okey dokey," said Arthur. "We can do that."

"Then . . ." I closed my eyes. I thought that this moment deserved a trumpet fanfare, or at least a drum roll. But there was only the sound of my pounding heart.

"I wish I were Tiffany Tupperman."

!

"HELP!" I was driving a small sports car and the road was going by me so fast that everything was a blur.

I looked at the speedometer and found the car was going seventy miles an hour.

"What's the matter, Tiff?" asked a boy sitting beside me. "Isn't this great?"

In an instant I realized that I was in Tiffany's red Trans Am, in Tiffany's body, with Tiffany's boyfriend next to me. Under ordinary circumstances I might be thrilled to be alone in a car with the extremely handsome Ned Bayer.

But I don't know how to drive.

"We're going to die!" I screamed. "Do something."

"What's wrong?" he asked. "If you're afraid of getting a ticket, slow down."

"I don't know how to—" Before I could finish the sentence I found my hand grasping the stick shift, and both feet pressing pedals to the floor. I have no idea how I did it, but in a matter of seconds the car slowed down and I pulled it over to the side of the road.

I sat there, trembling, trying to catch my breath. I could feel Ned's eyes boring into me. I was almost afraid to turn and face him.

If I did, who would he see? Did I have Tiffany Tupperman's face or did I only have her body and her driving ability?

I swallowed hard and peered into the rearview mirror.

Good grief. I really was Tiffany Tupperman. Except for a part of my mind that knew I was Jean Warren. But if I had become Tiffany, why was I still aware that I used to be Jean?

If I ever reversed this wish, I was going to ask Arthur a lot of questions.

Ned moved closer to me and put his arm around my shoulders. "I've been thinking about you all day," he said. He kissed my ear.

I jerked my head away. No one had ever kissed my ear before. In fact, except for relatives, no male over the age of nine had ever kissed any part of my head before.

"Maybe I distracted you while you were driving, right,

Tiff?" He grinned. "I have that effect on women. I guess you wanted to get to our favorite place."

He put his hands on my cheeks and pressed his lips against mine. He stuck his tongue in my mouth.

"Ick!" I yelled. "Don't do that!"

"Why not?" He sounded mystified.

"I don't like to kiss that way."

He looked shocked. "Since when?"

"Since—uh—very recently."

I could have told him that I'd only known him for about three minutes, but he was confused enough already. Which made two of us. Because if I was Tiffany, shouldn't I love him? Wouldn't I want him to kiss me?

Apparently we had a special spot where we went for serious snuggling.

"I don't get it," he grumbled. "You're not yourself at all."

"This is true," I agreed.

He grinned. "Uncle Ned can fix that with his miracle make-out therapy." He reached for me again. He stroked my hair and nuzzled my neck. I felt my pulse shoot up, but I don't know whether it was love or fear.

Ned was awfully good-looking, but I was awfully inexperienced. What did he expect from Tiffany? What was their usual passion pattern?

He moved his hands down my shoulders and pulled me against him. He kissed my lips again, but this time he kept his mouth closed.

It didn't feel bad. I was still very tense, but I was beginning to enjoy myself a little.

"There we go," he whispered. "That's my girl." He leaned over and pushed the car door open. "Let's go under our tree."

"Our tree?"

He came around to my side of the car. He helped me out and, holding my hand, led me across the deserted road toward a giant weeping willow.

I knew it was time to be nervous again.

"Uh—listen, Ned. I have to go home."

"But you told your mom you'd be late."

"I did? Well, it's pretty late already. Gosh, look at the time." I pointed to my wrist, which, unfortunately, did not have a watch on it.

He folded his arms across his chest. "I don't know what's going on with you, Tiff, but whatever it is, I don't like it. Do you want to be with me or not? Just tell me where I stand."

What should I tell him? I looked down at my feet. I was wearing nifty red tights and purple socks. I took a moment to admire how nice my legs looked.

"Well?" Ned said.

Considering that I had no idea what Ned and Tiffany did under that tree—all right, I had some idea—the safest move would be to get back into the car and speed away.

"I think we'd better go home, Ned."

"Now?"

I nodded. "Now."

"So that's how it is," he said nastily. "Okay, fine. I thought we meant something to each other but I guess I was wrong."

He turned his back on me and walked across the road to the car.

I followed. He sat down in the passenger seat.

I took a deep breath and got behind the wheel again.

Jean Warren didn't know Tiffany's address, but we got home somehow. I mean, Tiffany got home. I parked the Trans Am in the driveway and almost automatically walked through the garage and into the kitchen.

"Tiffany Tupperman!" A blond woman shouted at me. "This is the last straw. You were supposed to start dinner at five o'clock. Where have you been for the last three hours?"

"Uh—I'm not sure." It was the truth. I knew where I'd been for the past half hour, but not before.

"I walk in the house," she ranted, "not one bit of preparation is done, I have a seven-thirty appointment with a client, and you don't know where you've been for the last three hours."

"I'm really sorry . . . Mom."

"You're going to be sorrier," she said. "YOU. ARE. GROUNDED."

"Grounded?" I cried.

"For the rest of this week you're coming straight home from school. No clubs, no car, no Ned, no *nothing*."

"But Mrs.—I mean, Mom—"

"Don't you 'but Mom' me," she shrieked. "This time you're going to learn your lesson for good. You're grounded. Go to your room and stay there until the pizza I have to order is delivered."

This was terrible. I wanted to tell her I wasn't really her daughter. I wanted to tell her this was a mistake. I wanted to tell her not to get any anchovies on the pizza.

If I said a genie had transformed me into her daughter, she might ground me forever. And for all I knew Tiffany Tupperman loved anchovies.

What lousy luck, I thought, as I trudged up the stairs.

I finally get to be Tiffany Tupperman and I lose my boyfriend and my freedom in one afternoon.

I had no trouble finding my room. Being incarcerated in there wasn't exactly like being locked up in Alcatraz. There was a small color TV, a VCR, a stereo, an exercycle, and a walk-in closet that was bigger than Richie's room.

There was peach carpeting, white wicker furniture, and a cushioned window seat. It was a very plush cell.

But so what? Jeannie Warren could use the family VCR and listen to music anytime she wanted. And she never had the slightest urge to exercycle.

The whole idea of being Tiffany Tupperman was to learn how it felt to be liked, to be popular. I wasn't going to get that experience stuck in this room. And apparently I wasn't going to get out of this room until tomorrow morning—except to eat some pizza.

I could tough it out until tomorrow, sleeping here just one short night. I could go to school the next day and be Tiffany, and if I liked it, I could be Tiffany whenever I wanted to.

If I didn't like it—and right now I didn't like it one bit—I'd change back to Jean.

But I didn't have to wait, I reminded myself. Not

even one night. I could go home now, and wish to be Tiffany again tomorrow morning.

"I wish I were Jean again," I said. "And safe in my own house," I added hastily.

Nothing happened.

"I wish I were Jean Warren and safe in my own house," I repeated.

Nothing. I looked at my elegant prison. My palms started to feel moist. Little beads of sweat formed over my upper lip.

I looked in the full-length mirror on the inside of the closet door and started to shiver. I was Tiffany Tupperman, not Jean Warren, and this was my room, and there were my clothes, but I knew I wasn't Tiffany Tupperman and this was the scariest thing that had ever happened to me.

"Arthur," I whispered, "aren't you listening? I want to be me again. I don't feel right this way."

But of course Arthur wasn't listening.

Arthur wasn't here.

Arthur was at Jean Warren's house, inside a magic lantern that only Jean Warren knew about.

And if I was Tiffany Tupperman, who was Jean Warren?

Five

I woke up the next morning in a cotton nightshirt I couldn't remember putting on, in a bed I couldn't remember getting into.

I looked in the mirror over my dresser. I thought I looked pretty good for a person in a cotton nightshirt.

I went to my closet to choose an outfit. Without thinking about it, I reached for a black leather skirt with a matching jacket and a yellow shirt.

I pulled some underwear from a drawer and noticed that there was a white telephone on the table next to my bed.

Didn't I want to call someone? I was sure that there had been a phone call I'd needed to make last night, but I hadn't spotted the phone.

How silly. I must have known I had a phone. This was my room, these were my clothes, that was my phone. I was just a little groggy.

"Tiffany!" my mother called. "Breakfast."

I finished dressing. I checked myself out in the mirror.

Perfect. But somehow it was as if I were looking at myself for the first time. The clothes, the hair, the shape of the eyes . . . did I really look like this?

Silly Billy, I told myself. Who else would I look like? Any minute now eerie music was going to start—*ooohh-eeee-ooohh*—and I would turn back into Jean.

Turn back into Jean!

Of course I didn't look like myself. I wasn't Tiffany Tupperman, I was Jean Warren.

I felt almost faint. I was beginning to forget some of my Jean Warren memories. Would I become more and more Tiffany Tupperman until I forgot Jean Warren completely?

"Tiffany!" A male voice bellowed up the stairs. My father, I supposed. I meant, Tiffany's father. I was Jean. I had to remember that.

"Coming!"

I walked downstairs and followed the smell of coffee until I reached the kitchen.

Nice house, I thought. But not mine.

"Hi—Daddy." I took a not-very-wild guess that the man at the table was Tiffany's father.

"Good morning," he said. He was holding a coffee mug in his hand. He raised it in my direction. He looked nice.

"Your mother tells me I'm driving you to school this morning. No car for a while, eh?"

"You don't have to drive me." I tried to sound brave and trustworthy. "I can walk."

To my real house, I thought, to reverse this crazy wish.

They both gaped at me. "Three miles?" they said.

Oops. "Well, I don't want to put you to any trouble, Daddy."

"Oh, no," Mrs. Tupperman said bitterly, "but you don't care how much trouble you put *me* to."

"I'm sorry," I said. I sat down at the table. I guessed I wouldn't be able to do anything about being Tiffany until after school.

As long as I remember I'm really Jean, I told myself, why shouldn't I finally find out what it's like to be the popular Tiffany Tupperman?

It was hard to remember that I was Jean once I got to school. Almost everybody who passed me called, "Hi, Tiffany," or stopped to tell me something. I felt like a celebrity.

I *was* a celebrity. I was Tiffany Tupperman.

I liked it. I liked it very much. I'd never had the experience of being popular, and sometimes I wondered, was it really all that great being liked by a huge number of people?

It was. It was positively exhilarating.

I didn't want to keep reminding myself that I was Jean. Now I remembered what it felt like being Jean. Did I really want to change places with my old self again?

Ned acted very cool toward me. I wondered whether he'd still be angry at Tiffany if I was Jean again.

The rest of the morning did not go very well. I was

surprised to find myself going to Tiffany's classes automatically, without any uncertainty about where to go next.

It was like when I got dressed that morning—I just knew what to wear. It was strange that I knew how to get to her classes, but didn't know enough to pass the pop quiz in history, the sequential math test, or the oral report for speech.

Three zeros in one day must be some kind of school record. If Mrs. Tupperman found out about them, Tiffany could end up grounded for life.

By lunchtime I had decided that I really had to turn myself back into Jean. My plan was to cut out of school, head for my house—that is, Jean's house—and light the lamp.

But what, I wondered, if I was already there? Maybe I didn't go to school today. Maybe I didn't even exist! Maybe there was no Jean Warren anymore.

If there was no Jean, there might be no lamp. If there was no magic lamp, there was no way to undo my new identity.

I would have to remain beautiful, beloved, exquisitely dressed, one-hundred-percent-grounded Tiffany Tupperman for the rest of her/my life.

What a horrible prospect.

At eleven-thirty, instead of going to the lunchroom, I headed out the main entrance of the high school and started home.

If my calculations were right, and if I was remembering everything correctly, at eleven-thirty, my mother—Mrs.

Warren—should be at the library. My mother is a librarian. She's supposed to work from noon to five, but she always goes in early to read.

Richie would be at school, my father would be at his accounting office, accounting.

All I had to do was break into the house and get the lamp.

There was a broken basement window that my parents had been meaning to get fixed for two years. The lock didn't work and the wooden frame was rotted.

I must have nagged them once a week about getting that window fixed. It was an open invitation to burglars, I told them. They said, only to midget burglars.

They kept agreeing that they should get a new window, but they just never seemed to get around to it.

For reasonably sensible people they were pretty careless about domestic security. Now, of course, I was glad they'd never gotten the window fixed.

I'm not a midget, but I thought I had a good chance of getting myself through the window. My shoulders would be the hardest part, but the rest of me is narrow enough.

I looked around to make sure that none of the neighbors would spot me. It was quiet.

I squatted down in front of the window. I pulled at the frame. Nothing happened. Even though the wood looked crumbly, I couldn't get the window to open.

It was too bad I didn't have a set of burglar tools. It was too bad the window opened out instead of in. I got down on my knees and tugged at both ends of the frame.

The crumbly part almost dissolved under my fingers.

43

But the window didn't budge.

I finally realized that the only way I was going to get it open was by breaking one of the panes so I could pull the window toward me from the inside.

I would make some noise, but I had to risk it. Once I got the lamp, I could be out of this mess in an instant.

I glanced one more time at the houses on either side of ours, to make sure no one was watching me.

No one seemed to be. I took off my leather jacket and wrapped it around my arm and hand. I made a fist and smashed through the window. I reached inside through the broken pane and pulled the window toward me.

I brushed the shattered glass away and tried to climb into the basement. I put my legs through first, but I couldn't get the rest of me past the frame.

I wiggled out and tried again. This time I stuck my hand and arms through the window, but there was nothing inside to grab hold of. If I let myself drop I would land face-first on the concrete basement floor.

My parents were right, I thought. Only a midget could make it through here.

I was just trying to pull myself back out of the window when I heard a shrill voice behind me.

"Freeze, slimeball! I've got you covered."

Six

"Richie." I groaned. "Is that you?"

"How did you know my name?"

"Let me get up and I'll tell you."

"Okay," he said, "but one false move and you're lunchmeat."

I wriggled my way back out of the window frame and stood up.

Richie was wearing his Incredible Hulk pajamas. His nose was red and his feet were bare. He held a baseball bat on his shoulder.

"Who are you?" he asked.

"I'm a friend of your sister's," I said.

"My sister doesn't have any friends."

I wished he'd stop saying that. "Yes, she does," I answered. "She's very well-liked."

Richie gazed at me, his eyes narrow and suspicious. "Are you sure you know my sister?"

"Look," I improvised, "she knew you were home sick

today and she asked me to go to her house and pick up a book she needs for school."

"Why didn't she come herself?" Richie asked.

A reasonable question. I tried to think of a reasonable answer.

"She had to help a teacher with something," I said. "And I had this free period."

"Well . . ." Richie hesitated. And no wonder. We'd been drilled in dealing with strangers since the time we were babies. If Richie did let me in the house, he ought to be punished.

"Your sister told me what a smart, helpful brother you are," I coaxed.

"I'm calling the cops," Richie said. "I don't think you ever met my sister."

"All right, all right," I said. "She told me you were a sleazy little worm, but I thought you'd be mad if I said that."

"Come on in," Richie said. "Her room's on the third floor."

He followed me up the stairs, dragging the bat behind him so it thunked against each step.

Even before I went into the room I could see the lamp.

"Oh, good! It's still here," I said.

"What's here?" Richie asked.

"The lamp," I said happily. "What a relief."

A stream of blue smoke rose from it.

"Great, it's still lit! Arthur!" I said. "I don't want this wish anymore. Reverse it!"

!

I was upside down. Richie was upside down. We were
standing on the ceiling. So was all the furniture. If the
walls of my attic room hadn't been sloped, we might not
have known we were reversed.

"That's not what I meant at all!" I shouted. "And you
know it. Stop fooling around. Turn everything back."

!

We were back on the floor again.

Richie started to say something, then stopped. He
looked dazed.

"Now, make me Jean again."

!

I was alone in my room. Tiffany was gone. Richie
was gone. Arthur was leaning over the lamp to light his
cigar.

I sank down onto my bed.

"Arthur," I said, "that was awful."

"Being upside down?" he asked. "It's very good for
you. It improves circulation to the brain."

"No! Being Tiffany was awful."

"Why?"

"For one thing," I began, "she was grounded. I couldn't
do anything."

"Bad timing," Arthur said.

His or mine? I wondered.

"And for a while I nearly forgot I was me."

"Well, here you are, so there's no harm done," said Arthur.

"When I was Tiffany," I asked, "was Tiffany me?"

"No."

"But if I was Tiffany who was being me?"

He shrugged. "How should I know?"

"What do you mean?" I cried. "You must know. You're the one doing the magic."

"Hold on," said Arthur. "I'm a genie, not a philosopher. You're raising all kinds of complicated epistemological stuff."

"Epis—what?"

"Forget it." Arthur blew smoke rings toward me. "Why don't you just make another wish?"

"I'm afraid to make another wish," I said. "They don't seem to come out the way I expect."

"That's because you aren't specific enough," he said. "I warned you about that, didn't I?"

"What if I want to undo a wish and I don't have the lamp? How would I get home?"

"That could be a problem," Arthur said.

"Maybe I should take the lamp with me whenever I wish for something."

"That might work." Arthur floated around my room, flicking blue cigar ash with his pinkie.

"What do you mean, it *might* work?" I demanded. "You should know whether it will work or not."

"How can I tell?" Arthur said irritably. "Times change. I haven't been out for thirty-three years."

"Great," I grumbled. "Just great. What about when I was Tiffany? Did I really make Ned mad at her? And Mrs. Tupperman too? Did a whole day pass while I was being her?"

Arthur pulled out a watch from the pocket of his vest. He studied it. He held it up to his ear. He shook it impatiently.

"I can't tell," he said. "It seems to have stopped in 1957."

"Arthur!" I wailed.

"Listen, don't blame me for shoddy workmanship," he said. "They don't make watches like they used to."

This was incredibly frustrating.

"All right." I tried to stay calm. "Richie was here when you reversed the wish. Will he remember?"

"It depends—and don't yell at me again!" Arthur warned. "Not if the Cloud of Mystification was operating."

"It must be operating right now," I said. "I'm completely mystified. I have to find out if Richie knows about you. If he starts making wishes it could mean the end of the civilized world as we know it."

I brooded for a moment. "I have to know what day it is too. How long have I been gone?"

Suddenly I had a brainstorm. "I wish," I said carefully, "I wish I had today's newspaper."

!

Instantly a large wad of pages appeared in my hand. I looked at the headlines. They were in Chinese.

49

"Funny, Arthur. Very funny." I dropped the paper to the floor and kicked it across the room.

"It was the first one that came to hand," he said. "How am I supposed to know you can't read Chinese?"

"There's got to be an easier way to find out what day it is," I muttered.

"Good thinking," he said. "Why not ask someone human?"

"I will."

"Fine. Now, do you want to wish for anything else?"

"Not right now," I said. "I'm still not sure what happened during my last wish."

"Okey dokey." Arthur spun around till he was a whirlwind of blue smoke and swirled into the lamp. I put the lid on and breathed a sigh of relief.

It was good to be home.

Seven

Being a sane, sensible person, I decided that it might be wise to refrain from making major, life-changing wishes until I was certain I would get the wish I wanted.

After all, turning into Tiffany Tupperman hadn't worked out well at all. And the following day, when I was myself again, four teachers asked me for the homework assignments I hadn't done when I was Tiffany.

That afternoon I summoned Arthur from the lamp. I would start with something surefire and specific. It was a minor wish, but it could save me a lot of trouble.

"I wish I didn't have to do my homework," I said.

"Okey dokey," said Arthur.

!

My books were gone. My notebook was gone. My desk was gone.

51

The lamp was sitting on the floor of my room. I looked around. There was no paper, nothing to write with, nothing to study.

I sighed.

"Arthur, do you do these things on purpose?"

"What things?" he asked.

"Are you trying to teach me something, like it's best to accept what you are instead of trying to make your life better? I mean, are you here to show me that wishes are overrated and happiness is in your own backyard?"

Arthur's bushy black eyebrows knitted together. "I hardly know you," he said. "Why should I want to teach you anything?"

"Every time I wish for something you manage to louse it up."

"I beg your pardon," Arthur said huffily. "*I* louse it up? I'm only the genie. You're the one who makes the wish. I warned you to be specific."

"Okay, okay. Specific," I said. "First, bring back my books and my desk. And anything else that was in this room before I made my last wish."

!

"Thank you."

"You're welcome," said Arthur. His voice was chilly.

"Now . . ." I closed my eyes and tried to word my wish so that Arthur couldn't possibly make a mistake. "I wish that all my homework were already done. The makeup work, and today's homework. I wish it were done."

!

"It's done," Arthur said.

A small sheaf of papers rested on top of my loose-leaf. I looked through them. Sure enough, a page of math problems was done, another page was filled with irregular French verbs, there was a theme on *The Catcher in the Rye,* and a list of diseases you could get from smoking. Arthur must have resented doing that one. It was a health assignment.

"Thank you, Arthur!" I said. "This is great! And all in my own handwriting, too."

"You're quite welcome." He still sounded huffy. "Although you didn't *specify* that the work be done in your own handwriting."

"I guess I have a lot to learn about wish making," I said humbly.

"Indeed," he said.

"There's something else I want to know," I said. "Richie doesn't remember me breaking into the house yesterday. And the window is just the way it was before I smashed it. How can that be?"

"The Cloud of Mystification," Arthur said.

"You said that yesterday," I remembered. "What is it?"

"It protects the wisher and the lamp," he said. "The final outcome of the wish is accepted by those around the wisher without question. It is as if things were always the way they are wished unless the wish is terminated. Then things are the way they were before the wish."

"That's a little hard to follow," I said.

"Don't worry about it." He sounded friendlier now. "No one but the wisher and the genie is aware of the process of wishing and wish fulfillment."

"Why is that?" I asked.

"Beats me," said Arthur.

That was the main problem with having a genie. There were a hundred questions I wanted to ask Arthur, but every time he answered a question it raised a hundred new questions.

The wishing business seemed pretty risky. You never knew whether you would end up in a speeding car, or have to shovel snow out of your bedroom.

I really needed to talk to someone. Maybe I should have asked my mother about this. Or Aunt Jean. But I had a funny feeling that if my parents knew the power of the lamp, they might take it away from me. And if Aunt Jean knew, she'd have to tell them.

I could understand that. Even if I had a daughter as mature and well-balanced as I am, I'd probably be edgy knowing she had the ability to undo creation.

I could lose my temper one day and zap North America off the map. It was a terrifying thought. What if I did something like that by accident?

The more I thought about it, the more nervous I was about wishing for anything. What if I made a wish like that and couldn't undo it?

And whose fault was it that my wishes didn't work

out? Was I to blame for sloppy wishing, or was Arthur a substandard genie?

That Friday Lynn told me that Ned still wasn't speaking to Tiffany and I told her that I had some incredibly weird news for her.

"Come home with me after school and stay for dinner," I urged.

"Is it your night to cook?" Lynn asked.

"What difference does that make? I'm going to show you something so unbelievable that you're going to forget about food completely."

"I doubt it," said Lynn. "I've never forgotten your Tofu Helper."

"All right, it is my night to cook. But I'm not making anything healthy," I assured her. "Just hot dogs."

"In that case I'd love to come and see something unbelievable," she said.

I decided not to tell her that the hot dogs were made of soybeans.

"This isn't funny, Jean." Lynn looked frightened. "You don't really expect me to believe that you were Tiffany Tupperman on Tuesday?"

"But I do. I was. I can prove it."

"No you can't," she said. "I went to the dance club meeting in the afternoon and Tiffany was there."

"I was only Tiffany till lunchtime," I said. "Then I came home and undid the wish. Tiffany was herself by the time you saw her."

Lynn looked as if she were about to burst into

tears. "I think we ought to tell your mother about this."

"Don't get upset," I said. "I'll show you that all of this is true. I'll make a wish for both of us."

I lit the lamp.

I watched Lynn's face as the cloud of blue smoke curled up out of the lantern and took Arthur's shape.

"What is that?" Lynn sounded as if she were choking. I knew it couldn't be the smoke, because it had no smell. She was terrified.

Nothing could really prepare you for Arthur, especially if you don't believe in magic lanterns.

"That's the genie," I said. "Don't be afraid. That's Arthur."

"What can I do for you?" Arthur asked. He flicked his cigar ash and crossed his blue arms over his chest.

"Oh, my God." Lynn sounded weak.

"I wanted to show Lynn you were real," I explained to Arthur.

"That's Lynn?" He pointed a smoky finger at her. She backed away.

I nodded. "That's Lynn."

"Okay. I'm real," said Arthur. "Can I go now?"

"No. I want to make a wish that Lynn and I can share, so—"

"No!" Lynn shook her head wildly. "No thanks. I believe—whatever you say. I don't want to wish for anything."

"Come on, Lynn," I said. "We'll take the lamp with

us so we can get right back again. Arthur, tell Lynn she shouldn't be afraid."

"You shouldn't be afraid," Arthur said.

"Are you kidding?" Her voice was several notes higher than usual. "You just told me everything that's gone wrong since you started wishing. If I'm not dreaming, and this is really happening, I don't want any part of it."

"Oh, Lynn." I sighed. "Don't you realize what we could do? I can wish for anything we want. *Anything*. How can you pass up an experience like this?"

"It's easy," said Lynn. "I'm a coward."

"There's really nothing to be frightened about," I said. "Much. I wish you'd change your mind."

!

"Okay," said Lynn. "What should we wish for?"

It took me a moment to figure out that Lynn had agreed with me because I wished she would. Before she could change her mind I said, "Let's wish for something you want. But let's not wish to be other people. I don't think Arthur has the hang of that yet."

"I beg your pardon," he said. "I've been granting wishes for nine centuries. How long have you been making wishes?"

"No offense," I said. "I know I'm new at this."

"You want to hear something silly?" Lynn said. "You're going to laugh at me, but I always wanted to be on that quiz show. You know, the one you think is so stupid."

"You mean *Name That Person*?"

She nodded. "I know you hate it, but I've always wanted to be on that show. I saw a woman win fifty thousand dollars last night."

"Wouldn't it be simpler," I said, "for me to wish for fifty thousand dollars and just give it to you? You could do that, couldn't you, Arthur?"

"I could do that," he agreed.

"But I want to *win* it. On *Name That Person.* The other way is no fun."

I didn't think being on the show would be any fun, either, but it was Lynn's wish.

My parents watched *Name That Person* too. I couldn't understand why. The questions were so easy you had to be an idiot to lose.

I watched once in a while, but there was just no challenge to it. I mean, they asked questions like, "He was a famous U.S. president in the thirties and forties. His initials were FDR. Name that person."

I mean, really.

"Okay," I said. "But we'll take the lamp with us to make sure we can get back. Or in case we lose."

"Why should we lose?" asked Lynn. "It's our wish, isn't it? Why can't we wish to win?"

"Where's the excitement in that?" I asked. "You'll already know you're going to win."

"That's exciting," Lynn said. "Wishing to win is sort of an insurance policy."

"Good thinking," said Arthur. "You have to be very specific about what to wish for. Some people are careless about that."

"All right," Lynn said. "We want to be winning contestants on *Name That Person*. Say it that way."

"Okay." I spoke very clearly. "I wish that Lynn and I could be winning contestants on *Name That Person*."

!

Eight

"Ooh, I can't believe it! I'm so *nervous*," Lynn said. We were standing backstage at what was obviously a television studio. "Aren't you nervous?"

"Not as long as I have the lamp," I said. "At least we'll be able to get out of this wish fast if Arthur screws up again."

"You're on next, girls." A blond woman carrying a clipboard pointed to the lamp. "Do you want to leave that thing back here with me?"

"No," I said. I tucked it under my arm. "I'd better hold onto it."

"A good-luck piece." She nodded. "I understand. Well, it's bigger than a rabbit's foot, but that's all right."

"The show is on tape, isn't it?" I asked. Even I was beginning to be nervous about being on television, though I couldn't care less about *Name That Person*.

"Yes, we're taping," the woman said. "But we don't

61

stop for anything unless the director tells us to. And you'll be in front of a live audience."

"Okay!" someone yelled. "Bring on the next team."

"That's you," the woman said. She patted us on our shoulders. "Good luck!"

The hostess of the show, Beverly Bright, escorted us onto the stage. The lights were hot and glaring, and Johnny Marshall and Beverly looked as if they had orange makeup on.

"Here are our new challengers, Johnny," Beverly said. "Say hi to Jean Warren and Lynn Shoemaker."

Beverly herded us over to Johnny. The audience cheered and clapped as if they were rooting for us to win.

I wondered if this show would ever be broadcast. Was any of this really happening? When we finished our appearance on *Name That Person,* would there be a tape somewhere with us on it?

"Hello, ladies." Johnny Marshall smiled. He had about ten more teeth than a normal person. "And welcome to *Name That Poison.*"

"Name that what?" Lynn asked.

Johnny went right on talking as if he hadn't heard her.

"These are our current champions." Johnny gestured toward the middle-aged couple opposite us. "Duane and Mary Cosgrove. They're pretty tough, but maybe you can dethrone them. Let's play *Name That Poison.*"

"Name that *what*?" Lynn repeated.

The audience clapped and whistled.

"Which of you girls will go first?" Johnny asked.

"She will." We each pointed to the other.

Johnny laughed heartily. "Come, come now, you know how the game is played. One of you has to start."

"I guess I'll go first," Lynn said.

"Okay. The first question is worth a thousand dollars, and it's for Lynn and Mary. Hands on buzzers, ring in when you know the answer. This plant, usually associated with Christmas, has whitish berries, which are poisonous. Name that poison!"

Lynn hit her buzzer. "*Phoradendron flavescens,* commonly known as mistletoe," she said.

"That's absolutely right!" Johnny shouted. "That's a thousand dollars for the challengers."

Lynn looked as surprised as I was. Well, we had wished to be winning contestants. Maybe it would be all right after all.

"The next thousand-dollar question goes to Jean and Duane. Listen carefully. This perennial herb grows in moist woodland areas. Its pea-sized blue berries are toxic. The Latin name of this poisonous plant is *Caulophyllum thalictroides.* Name that poison!"

Lynn turned to me hopefully. Mary turned to Duane hopefully. I couldn't look Lynn in the eye. I didn't have the faintest idea what *Caulo*—whatever was.

"Time's almost up," Johnny said.

I stared down at the floor. The audience was silent.

"Time's up," Johnny announced. "No money on that one."

The audience sighed collectively. "Awww . . ."

"We'll try another question for two thousand dollars," said Johnny. "Ready, Lynn and Mary?"

Lynn put her finger on her buzzer.

"This plant contains the toxic alkaloid *hyoscyamine* throughout—"

Both buzzers went off.

Lynn looked at Johnny eagerly.

"That's a close one," he said. "But our judges say Lynn hit her button first. Name that poison, Lynn."

"*Atropa belladonna,*" Lynn said.

"That's absolutely right!" shouted Johnny.

"Ooohh!" Lynn squealed and jumped up and down in her excitement. She looked positively idiotic.

"That's two thousand dollars more for the challengers!"

Lynn screeched and hugged me. "Three thousand dollars!" she cried.

Duane and Mary looked worried.

I didn't know when Lynn had learned so much about poisons. Somehow Arthur must have given her the knowledge to be a winner on the show, even though he got the name of the show wrong. Maybe he'd given me some poison info too. After all, I had driven Tiffany's car when I didn't know how to drive.

"Now, for the five-thousand-dollar question."

Lynn grabbed my arm. "Put your finger on the buzzer," she whispered. She was so excited she couldn't stand still.

I clutched the magic lamp tighter and rested my finger on the buzzer.

"This tuberous rhizome is rich in calcium oxalate crystals and produces inflammation of the—"

Duane hit his buzzer. "Jack-in-the-pulpit," he said. "*Arisaema* in Latin."

"You're right!"

Lynn scowled at me as the audience cheered for Duane. "Come on," she whispered. "That was an easy one."

"Easy for you," I said, under my breath. "Let's get out of here."

"Not now," Lynn said. "Wait till we win the fifty thousand."

I didn't think we had a prayer of winning the fifty thousand dollars. We weren't even on the right show. If Arthur had screwed up this wish too, there was no guarantee that we'd win anything.

But I stayed there in the wish, on the stage, with the bright lights making me perspire, for what seemed an eternity.

I didn't answer one question. It was humiliating. I had never felt so stupid in my whole life. I wanted to hide. The audience groaned every time I missed a question. Which was every time I was asked a question.

"Concentrate," Lynn hissed.

"I *hate* this," I whispered.

"Just a little while longer," Lynn said.

Fortunately Duane missed a few of the questions that I couldn't answer. Finally there was a loud blare of trumpets.

"And now," said Johnny Marshall, "we reach the top of the *Name That Poison* prize ladder. Fifty thousand dollars!"

The audience screamed. Lynn clapped her hands together eagerly. Mary and Duane looked tense.

"Here's the situation," Johnny said. "Lynn and Jean, the challengers, have successfully answered the forty-thousand-dollar question. If one of them can answer the next question they win fifty thousand dollars and are declared our new *Name That Poison* champions."

"Ooohh," Lynn moaned.

"But if they miss, Mary and Duane will have a shot at the question. If the Cosgroves can answer the fifty-thousand-dollar question, they retain their championship and retire unbeaten."

"I can't stand it!" Lynn squealed. If she ever saw this show she'd be mortified. I knew I would be.

"The fifty-thousand-dollar question," Johnny announced, "is for Duane and Jean."

The audience groaned.

I felt my face turn red. Everyone knew by now that I was incredibly stupid about toxic substances, and the only way we would be able to win was if Duane couldn't answer.

I hugged the magic lamp to my chest.

Lynn crossed her fingers.

"Here we go," Johnny said. "There are three primary groups of plant glycosides that yield toxic products on hydrolysis. One group is called cyanogenetic, in which the poisonous product is hydrocyanic acid or prussic acid—"

Duane hit his buzzer. Lynn pushed my hand down on my buzzer.

I couldn't stand it for another second.

"I hate this show!" I wailed.

There was a collective gasp from the members of the audience. Then a low, grumbling sound, as if they wanted to show me they didn't like me anymore.

"I want to go home!"

!

We were back in my room. I was holding the lamp.
Arthur was sitting cross-legged on my desk, smoking.
"What is the matter with you?" Lynn demanded. "We
were just going to win the fifty thousand dollars!"

"No we weren't," I said. "Didn't you notice we were
on the wrong show?"

"But I knew the answers anyway," Lynn said.

I glared daggers at Arthur. He wouldn't look me in
the eye.

"We only said we wanted to be winning contestants,"
I pointed out. "We didn't say how much money we wanted
to win."

Arthur examined his blue fingernails.

"Let's do it again," Lynn said eagerly. "But this time
we'll—"

A stream of blue-smoke question marks puffed toward
us from Arthur's cigar.

"This time we could be on another show," Lynn said.
"Or maybe we could be movie stars or end world hunger
or—"

Telling Lynn had been a mistake, I realized. Now
she'd want to make wishes all the time. How could she
resist?

The smoke question marks formed a small blue cloud.
Lynn didn't seem to notice when the cloud enveloped her
head.

"What's happening?" I asked Arthur.

"A genie cannot serve two masters," he said. "After she emerges from the Cloud of Mystification she won't remember any of this."

"Well, I just hope you're doing *this* right," I said.

"I'm sorry," Arthur said. "Maybe if you could speak more clearly next time . . ."

The cloud passed over Lynn's head and floated back toward the lamp.

"I guess our TV debut won't ever be shown," I said.

"What are you talking about?" asked Lynn.

"No, it won't," said Arthur. "Everything is back the way it was."

"It wasn't a real show anyway," I said.

"What wasn't a real show?" Lynn looked confused. I guessed she couldn't see or hear Arthur because she'd been zapped with the Cloud of Mystification. It was just as well.

"Anything else?" Arthur stood with one blue-smoke toe on the edge of the lamp.

"I think you've done enough," I said.

"Okey dokey."

"What did I do, Jean?" Lynn asked. "Are you mad at me?"

"Not you," I said.

Arthur twirled himself down into the lamp. I put the lid on.

"What show were you talking about?" Lynn asked. "What did I miss?"

"*Name That Poison*," I said.

"Oh, cut it out." Lynn laughed. "You know perfectly well it's *Name That Person*."

"Yeah, right," I said. "I guess I'd better get started on those hot dogs."

"I'll help," Lynn said. "You know, I've always wanted to be on that show, but I don't suppose they'd take teenagers. . . ."

Nine

It was so hard to understand. Lynn had told me that Ned wasn't speaking to Tiffany, even though she kept trying to corner him in school.

That must have meant that Ned was still angry at what I had done when I was Tiffany.

That didn't seem right if the Cloud of Mystification was working. And I knew it worked, because Lynn didn't remember anything about Arthur.

But the final outcome of my wish to be Tiffany was that I turned back into myself. So how come things weren't exactly the way they'd been before?

Two days later I got the last of my genie-generated homework assignments back. It was the theme on *The Catcher in the Rye.*

Mr. Kellogg handed it back to me with a little shake of his (incredibly handsome) head. "This is a disappointment," he said, "coming from you."

There was a D circled in red at the top of the page.

"It sounds as if you never read the book," he said.

"I did read the book," I said. "I really did."

"I can't tell that from this paper," he said.

I lowered my eyes to the top of my desk. I thought I might cry if I had to look into his deep blue, gorgeous, reproachful eyes any longer.

That D was the lowest grade I'd ever gotten on a writing assignment in my whole life. I can't say it came as a complete shock. The other assignments that Arthur did for me got F's.

("You didn't *specify*!" Arthur said later. "You just said you wanted them done. You didn't say they should be done *correctly*.")

I stuffed *The Catcher in the Rye* theme into my loose-leaf as Mr. Kellogg walked back to his desk.

I told myself that it was only a temporary problem. After school I would tell Arthur to wipe out that D and change it to an A.

But Arthur could do more than that, I realized.

Arthur could get me Mr. Kellogg.

Another problem with high school is that it's filled with teenage boys. And teenage boys bore me silly. They admire big muscles and cool cars and sexy girls and they have small minds, no couth, and dumb girlfriends.

That's probably why I was so passionate about Mr. Kellogg.

At my age it was inevitable that I would find some member of the opposite sex attractive. That's just part of human development. Since most of the high-school boys I know are about as appealing as raw liver, I must have turned to Mr. Kellogg out of desperation.

Whatever the original reason for my deep and profound attraction to Mr. Kellogg, it was not merely an ordinary adolescent crush.

I've seen girls with adolescent crushes throwing themselves into his path. I could never act as silly as they do.

First of all, my love for Mr. Kellogg had nothing to do with his incredible good looks.

Okay, okay, maybe it did. The main thing, though, was that we shared similar intellects.

What teenage boy could match Mr. Kellogg for sophistication, experience, and intelligence?

Second, Mr. Kellogg was the only teacher I have ever been in love with. I didn't have a whole string of unrequited romances with older men. In fact, before now I hadn't had romantic feelings for anyone.

As realistic and mature as I am, I couldn't help fantasizing just a little about Mr. Kellogg. Every time he spoke to me I imagined him saying something that had nothing to do with English.

Something like, "Haven't you guessed my real feelings for you, Jean?"

Or, "You're so different from all the other girls. I noticed that the first time I saw you."

For someone who hadn't believed in Santa Claus or the Tooth Fairy, this was a severe attack of imagination.

But now, at last, my fantasy would come true. All I had to do was light the magic lamp.

Arthur would take care of the rest.

And this time he'd do it *right!*

I couldn't wait to get home from school that day. I made some lame excuse to Lynn for running off without her, and jogged most of the eight blocks to my house.

I couldn't explain why I wanted to get home so fast. I told myself that if she could only remember Arthur and my magic lamp, she'd sympathize.

I was surprised to see my mother's car in the driveway. She usually doesn't get home till five-thirty.

I went inside. My mother and Richie were talking in the kitchen.

"How come you're home?" I asked, walking in on them.

"I live here," said Richie. "What's your excuse?"

My mother grinned. "Plumbing problems at the library. We closed early."

For the first time I saw what she had in her hands.

I screamed. "What are you doing to my lamp?"

She was holding it over the sink and it was covered with something that looked like pink toothpaste. An odor of rotten eggs stank up the room.

"Just polishing it," she said calmly. "It was so tarnished."

"I liked it tarnished!" I cried. "I liked it just the way it was. If it was supposed to look polished Aunt Jean would have polished it."

I grabbed it from her. "You probably got the candle all wet!"

"I'm sorry," my mother said. "I was curious to see

how it would look shiny. I never thought you'd be so upset about it."

I started wiping the polish off with paper towels. I looked inside the lamp. "The candle is dripping wet."

"It'll dry," she said. "And you can always get another candle."

"I'm not so sure about that," I said.

"You have to rinse that off after you wipe it," my mother said. "Otherwise—"

"Okay, I'll rinse it off." I put the lid on and carefully used a sponge soaked in cold water to wash away the polish.

I dried the lamp with a dish towel. I was too shaken to talk. As I walked upstairs I heard Richie say something rude about me. My mother shushed him.

If the candle was wet, how could I light the lamp? I could try to replace the candle. It was about two inches high and kind of stubby, and it seemed to burn very slowly. It was hardly any smaller now than when I first got the lamp.

It had to be unique. It was magic.

I found a box of candles in the linen closet. I would try one of those, even though I knew it was hopeless.

I went up the third flight of stairs to my room. I closed the door behind me.

I put the lamp on my desk. I took the lid off. The wick was drooping. The candle was dripping.

I tried to dry it off with a tissue. Just getting my fingers inside the lamp was hard, and the wick stayed wet even after the candle was fairly dry.

I couldn't get the candle out, either. It wouldn't budge and I couldn't get my fingers around it firmly because the opening was too narrow.

"Arthur," I whispered, "where are you? Are you still in there?"

Of course Arthur didn't answer. I was sure it was futile, but I tried to light the magic candle. The match fizzled and went out. Once. Twice.

I wanted to scream. When would I be able to light the lamp again? How long does it take for the wick in a magic lamp to dry? This is not a problem they prepare you for in school.

I was so frustrated and helpless that I began pacing back and forth around my room. I'd waited almost a year for this moment—the moment when Mr. Kellogg would take me in his arms and swear eternal devotion.

And what do I get? A wet wick.

I heard Richie climbing up the stairs. He threw my door open and said, "Can I borrow your blow dryer?"

"Would you *please* knock before entering my room?" I growled.

Richie tapped on the door. "Knock knock. Can I borrow your blow dryer?"

"What for?"

"I have to dry off my sneakers. Mom put them in the washing machine yesterday and they're not dry yet."

"I guess you can use it," I said. "Just don't break it."

"Thanks. I won't break it."

I grabbed him by the shoulders. "*Dry off your sneakers!* What a great idea!"

"Thanks." He looked puzzled.

"You're a genius," I said. "And a dear, sweet brother. And you can borrow my blower just as soon as I dry off this candle."

I raced to the bathroom and got my hair dryer from the counter. I sprinted back to my room. Richie was leaning against the door looking dazed. I guess the "dear, sweet brother" part confused him.

I plugged the dryer in and aimed the nozzle inside the lamp. I turned on the blower.

"How long will this take?" Richie asked. "I have a soccer game."

"I don't know. If you're in that much of a hurry borrow Mom's."

"What happened to dear, sweet genius me?"

I pulled the nozzle out of the lamp. I didn't want to risk melting the candle with the heat from the blower.

I tried to feel the wick. I couldn't tell if it was dry or not. There wasn't enough of it to feel. I turned the dryer down to low.

"Je-ean, come *on*."

I'd been patient long enough. By this time I should have been nestled in Mr. Kellogg's arms, exchanging words of endearment and a number of serious kisses—not standing here trying to blow-dry a candle with a pesty ten-year-old harassing me.

"OUT!" I shouted. "This dryer is mine and you can't have it yet!"

"You don't have to scream," he whined.

"Yes I do!" I screamed. "You're still here, aren't you?"

"Not anymore," he said. He headed for the stairs. "So long, elephant breath."

"Good riddance, gnat brain."

He stomped down the stairs.

I turned off the blow dryer. My fingers trembled as I struck a match.

I stretched my fingers to reach the wick. For a moment nothing happened. Then there was a little puff of smoke, and just as the match burned down to my nails, the wick caught the flame.

I dropped the match inside the lamp.

A small spiral of blue smoke curled out of the lamp.

"Thank goodness." I felt weak with relief. The thought that I would never be able to use the lamp again had terrified me.

Maybe I ought to wish for everything I could think of at one time, before the magic wore off.

Arthur took shape in the center of the room, hovering between my bed and the desk.

"I'm here," he said.

"I'm glad," I said. "I've been thinking. I want to consolidate my wishes."

"What do you mean?"

"Instead of wishing for one thing at a time, I want to wish for a whole bunch of stuff at the same time. It's more efficient that way."

Arthur blew a puff of smoke toward me. It turned into a plus sign as it drifted past my nose.

"You can't," he said. "Only one wish at a time."

"Why?"

He shrugged his blue shoulders. "That's the rule. I guess there would be too many variables. You have to maintain some stability."

"I don't get it," I said.

"How do you know what you'll want next?" he said. "You have to see the effect of each wish before you ask for another one."

"That sounds logical."

"I'm glad you think so," said Arthur, "because I just now made it up. I don't know why you have to wish for one thing at a time. I only know that that's the way it works."

"All right," I said. "If I get this wish my fondest dream will come true, so I suppose I can wait for the other wishes."

"Okey dokey," said Arthur. "Shoot."

"I'm going to word it right this time," I said. "I don't want any mistakes on this one."

"Take your time," Arthur said. "I've got all century."

"I wish . . . I wish Mr. Kellogg—Mr. *Gerald* Kellogg, my English teacher—loved me. I wish he were holding me in his arms right this minute."

"Okey—"

"No, wait! I have to take the—"

"—dokey."

!

Ten

"—lamp!"

"Are you having a good time, honey?"

I felt a little dizzy. And no wonder. Mr. Kellogg was waltzing me around the school gym. Red-and-silver hearts and cupids dangled from the rafters. The floor was crowded with other couples, all students.

It must be Valentine's Day. Strange. It had been May only a moment ago.

But how romantic. How perfect. I sighed and pressed my cheek against Mr. Kellogg's shoulder. I didn't know how to waltz. I didn't know how to dance at all before this moment.

He looked down at me fondly. "Well, I'm having a good time. For your sake I'm sorry that Ned doesn't know how to waltz. But for my sake I'm glad."

"Ned who?" I gripped Mr. Kellogg's hand a little tighter.

"Ned Bayer. Your boyfriend."

My boyfriend?

Again?

Something was wrong. Mr. Kellogg was supposed to be my boyfriend. Ned Bayer was Tiffany's boyfriend.

I wasn't holding the lamp. I had forgotten to take it with me. With Arthur's track record I had a feeling I was in big trouble.

"Don't tell me that one dance with your old daddy made you forget your beau?" Mr. Kellogg twirled me around the bandstand.

"*Daddy?*" I shrieked. "My old *daddy?*"

"And proud of it, too," he said. "You're the prettiest girl here."

I looked up at him. "My old dandy," I said. "That's just daddy. I mean, my old daddy, that's just—oh, forget about it."

Round and round we waltzed. Mr. Kellogg—Daddy—kept telling me how terrific I looked and how delighted he was to be dancing with me.

I didn't say much. What I was thinking was unprintable. Arthur just had to be doing this on purpose. How could he get every single wish wrong by accident?

There's my luck. I get a genie and it's got a warped sense of humor.

And where was the lamp? How was I going to undo this screwy wish?

The music changed to a rock beat.

"May I cut in?" Ned Bayer tapped Mr. Kellogg on the shoulder.

"Go ahead," Mr. Kellogg said. "I'm too old for this one."

Ned grinned and danced me away. How come I kept ending up with him? Karma? Kismet? Coincidence?

"You don't really want to dance, do you?" he asked teasingly.

"Well . . ."

Did I know any dances besides the waltz?

"We don't have to dance." He whispered in my ear. "We could get some punch. Or go out to the parking lot for some fresh air. Or something."

He pulled me closer to him. It didn't feel terrible. I remembered how he had kissed me when I was Tiffany. I hoped that this time he would keep his tongue to himself, but except for that I had no objections.

"What about your girlfriend, though?"

"What girlfriend?" he said.

"Tiffany."

"Who's Tiffany?"

"Stop joking, Ned. I'm serious."

"Why are we talking about Tiffany?" he asked.

The music stopped but Ned didn't let go. That was fine with me. I wondered how he could be nervy enough to smooch me in front of my own father. Formerly my English teacher. Possibly Ned's English teacher.

The music started again.

"You want to dance?" he asked. "Or should we go outside?"

I only hesitated for a moment. "Outside."

I hoped Daddy wouldn't mind.

"It's chilly out here, isn't it?" Ned said.

"It usually is in February," I said.

We sat on the school steps. We weren't the only couple sitting on the steps. None of them were chatting.

Ned pulled my face toward his and kissed me. Only with his lips.

He put his arms around me. "Let's get in the car."

"Where should we go?" I asked.

"Nowhere," he said.

"Sounds good to me."

He led me to a car and helped me into the front seat. He put his hands on my shoulders underneath my coat. I raised my lips to meet his.

Maybe Arthur's mistake was going to turn out better than I thought. Maybe Arthur didn't make a mistake. Right now I was enjoying this wish a lot more than any of the others.

It was certainly better than real life.

"Penelope," Ned whispered.

Maybe it was a secret password we had.

"Penelope," I agreed. I squeezed his hand and snuggled against his suede jacket.

He looked down at me. "What?" he asked.

"What what?" I said.

This was not the high level of conversation that I was capable of, but who wanted to converse? It was beginning to feel awfully warm for February.

"Penelope?" he said softly.

Here we go again.

"Come on, Penelope, it's Valentine's Day."

Finally I caught on. *I* was Penelope.

I wondered briefly whether I wanted to stay in a wish where I'd have to be called Penelope.

Ned kissed my hair. "Relax, Penelope honey."

There are worse names than Penelope, I decided.

As someone who never had any reason to celebrate Valentine's Day I found this February 14 a bonanza. Kissing and hugging the real Ned was even more wonderful than my former fantasies about Mr. Kellogg. This was even better than the first time Ned kissed me.

"Don't you think we ought to stop?" I said reluctantly.

"Why? You know how I feel about you."

"Oh, sure," I said. "What about Tiffany?"

"Tiffany *who*?" He sounded exasperated.

"Tiffany Tupperman," I said. "Your girlfriend."

He let go of me and started to laugh. "Don't be dense," he said. "Tiffany Tupperman's in love with your father."

Discovering that Mr. Kellogg was my father was only slightly less disturbing than imagining Tiffany Tupperman as my stepmother.

"What's the matter?" Ned asked. "Didn't you know about it? Everyone else does."

"I guess the daughter is always the last to know." I was so unnerved I forgot all about kissing and hugging. First I had to check the roots of my twisted family tree.

"What about my mother?" I asked. "Doesn't she mind?" (Whoever she is.)

Ned looked as confused as I felt. "What's with you tonight? You don't have a mother. She's dead."

"Oh, right. Dead."

This was terrible. Not the Ned part, but the prospect of remaining in a wish where I might have to see Mr. Kellogg making out with Tiffany Tupperman.

Disgusting.

The sooner I got out of this wish the better. Once I was Jeannie again I wouldn't have Ned to kiss. But back in the real world Ned was still angry at Tiffany. There might be a ray of hope for me yet.

"I have to go home," I said. (Wherever that was.) I didn't know where I lived. I hoped Ned did. I hoped that the magic lamp would miraculously appear there.

"You're just not yourself tonight," Ned grumbled.

"Tell me about it."

Ned insisted on telling Mr. Kellogg we were leaving the dance early. Then Mr. Kellogg insisted on taking me home himself.

"I'm not sick," I said. "I just have a little headache."

I waited for him under a paper cupid while he went to get his coat. I already had mine on. If Ned Bayer was hopelessly smitten with me, I thought, maybe I shouldn't be so hasty about turning myself back into Jean Warren.

Mr. Kellogg came back with his coat on one arm and Tiffany on the other. "We'll drop Tiffany off first," he said. "Then we'll go straight home."

"I'm sorry you're not feeling well." Tiffany flashed a synthetic smile. "It's so nice of your father to drive me home. Lance is absolutely disgusting tonight."

"Boys will be boys," Mr. Kellogg said. "It seems as if

drinking until you throw up is a traditional rite of passage from boyhood to maturity."

He led us out the door and down the steps to the parking lot. We had to climb over several couples on the steps. I kicked someone by accident. Unfortunately it wasn't Tiffany.

Ned planted a brief good-night kiss on my cheek and walked off toward his own car.

"It's true," Tiffany said. "Real men don't have to drink to prove their masculinity." She looked adoringly at Daddy.

"That's very perceptive," he said. He tucked her arm under his.

I followed a little way behind them, which is why, when we got to Daddy's Volvo station wagon, Tiffany beat me to the front seat.

"Poor Penelope," she said. "You ought to stretch out in the back and try to get some sleep."

She sounded so insincere I wanted to smack her. But Mr. Kellogg seemed touched by the depth of her concern for me.

"That's a good idea." Mr. Kellogg slid into the driver's seat and slammed the door. "You just close your eyes and try to rest, dear."

Sure. Close my eyes so he and Tiffany can neck at red lights? Not a chance.

"It's nice of you to be so caring about Penelope," he said softly. The engine turned over and the car started to move.

"It's not easy," he went on, "raising a daughter alone."

"I understand," Tiffany said. Her voice dripped with fake compassion. "At this age a girl really needs a mother."

"You do understand, don't you?" He patted her arm.

What was the matter with him? I thought Mr. Kellogg was smart. But he was eating up Tiffany's act like salted peanuts.

I seethed in the backseat. Their voices grew lower.

". . . only a matter of time," he murmured.

". . . graduation," she said. "Then we two will be one. . . ."

"Well, three, really," he said.

Tiffany rested her head on his shoulder. "Whatever," she said.

The sooner I got out of this wish the better.

Eleven

Mr. Kellogg unlocked the door to his apartment. I tried not to look as if I'd never seen it before. The place didn't look very large. There were two built-in bookcases in the living room. I wanted to check out the titles, but Mr. Kellogg's daughter ought to know them already.

Everything was very tasteful. The colors were muted beiges, browns, and grays. I wondered if my mother—whoever she had been—had done the decorating herself.

"Are you feeling any better, dear?" Mr. Kellogg helped me off with my coat.

"Not much." I tried to sound pathetic. "If you could just help me to my room . . ." (So I won't have to try and find it.)

His forehead creased with concern. "Good idea. I'll get you settled and you can take an aspirin and try to sleep it off."

He put his arm around me and led me down a short hallway. There seemed to be only two bedrooms, and I wouldn't have had any problems guessing which was mine. I mean, Penelope's.

A canopy bed dominated the room. The canopy was fuchsia. The bedspread was fuchsia. The curtains were fuchsia. There wasn't a piece of furniture in that room with straight edges. There wasn't a piece of material in that room without ruffles.

Everything was white and gold and fuchsia. Except the small TV. That was pink plastic.

There were no bookshelves.

"Now, lie down and close your eyes," said Mr. Kellogg.

It was the only sensible thing to do in that room.

I sat on the edge of the bed while Mr. Kellogg got the aspirin. I looked around the room—much as it pained me to do so—hoping that the magic lamp would be there.

I didn't see it.

Mr. Kellogg came back with the aspirin and a glass of water. I took the aspirin and he leaned down and kissed me on the forehead.

How ironic. I'd wished so long for a relationship with Mr. Kellogg, and now that I had one, it was the wrong relationship.

"I hope you feel better in the morning, dear."

The only way I could feel better in the morning would be by not waking up in this room.

"Thank you, Daddy."

Mr. Kellogg tiptoed out of my room—I mean, Penelope's room. You couldn't hear a footstep on the deep, shaggy white rug. He closed the door.

Naturally I didn't really have a headache. The moment the door closed I jumped off the bed—which was much too soft—and walked over to the dressing table.

I looked into the mirror.

I screamed.

I didn't really faint. Even though Mr. Kellogg found me slumped over the ruffled dressing table, I didn't lose consciousness.

"Did you hit your head?" he asked, peering into my eyes. "Should I call the doctor?"

"No, I just slipped." He helped me to straighten up, and as I did, I caught sight of that creature in the mirror again.

She wasn't me. I mean, she wasn't Jean Warren. But that didn't surprise me. When I was Tiffany Tupperman I looked like Tiffany Tupperman. Now I looked—weird.

"What's the matter, Penelope?" Daddy asked. "Are you sure you don't have a concussion?"

I shook my head. The stranger in the mirror shook her head. It was covered with frizzy, strawberry-colored hair. There was a streak of purple over my right temple. I looked like a refugee from a punk disaster.

I was wearing a flimsy chartreuse camisole with thin straps and laces up the front. My skirt—what little there was of it—was electric pink.

How could Daddy have let me wear an outfit like that in public?

"I'm fine," I lied. "Honestly."

Mr. Kellogg was reflected in the mirror and I compared our faces, side by side. I didn't look the least bit like him. I must take after my mother, I guessed.

"I'm going right to sleep," I said.

I wondered if I'd ever sleep again.

"And my head feels better already."

"Well . . ."

He backed out the door and closed it behind him.

I leaned on the dressing table and stared at the girl in the mirror. She certainly wasn't ugly. In fact, she was much prettier than Jeannie Warren.

Her skin was pink and creamy and she was much curvier than I was. She looked like the kind of girl Ned Bayer might love.

I asked myself again if I should be in such a hurry to get out of this wish. After all, Mr. Kellogg—*Daddy*—would probably be thrilled to buy me a new wardrobe and get my hair de-punked.

It finally got through to me. Unless I found my magic lamp I would have no choice. That was scary. At least I had to try and find the lamp, and then make up my mind about who I wanted to be.

I started to explore the room. I opened three dresser drawers. Sweaters, underwear, nightclothes.

The desk was French provincial, white with gold stenciling with only two narrow drawers at the top.

I knew the lamp couldn't be in there, but I looked anyway.

Under the bed, inside the closet, beneath the skirt of the dressing table . . . I tried to be quiet while I searched, but I got more and more frantic as I scoured the room.

The magic lantern simply wasn't there.

I sank down on the bed and put my hand over my

eyes. Maybe I could make a wish without the lamp. Maybe Arthur could hear me here.

I remembered the morning, which seemed so long ago, when I'd wished for an Egg McMuffin and found myself holding one.

Then I remembered that I had tried to call Arthur when I was Tiffany Tupperman. It didn't work. Maybe I had to be in the same room as the lamp for Arthur to hear me.

There was nothing left to do but try. If I could turn back into Jean, I could come back here with the lamp and be Penelope whenever I wanted.

I squeezed my eyes tightly shut.

"I wish I were Jean Warren again."

?

"I wish I were Jean Warren again."

?

I didn't feel any different. I opened my eyes, even though I was afraid of what I would see.

Fuchsia and flounces. Ruffles 'R' Us. Penelope's room.

It was no place like home.

I tried to sleep. The night would pass more quickly if I was unconscious through most of it.

The bed was as mushy as a cream puff, the canopy

above me gave me claustrophobia, and those were only the minor problems.

It was a good thing I hadn't wished for world peace. With Arthur's sense of humor I probably would have set off a nuclear war.

The room looked a lot better with the lights out, but after an hour I knew I wouldn't sleep. I couldn't just lie there anymore. I switched on the bedside lamp. The little white clock on the night table said eleven.

I gazed around the room. I hadn't noticed before, but there was one—only one—book on the spindly legged desk.

And right next to it, a white, cordless telephone.

I knew what I had to do.

My hand was trembling as I picked up the phone.

I couldn't remember my number. I mean, Jean's number. I dropped the phone as if it were on fire.

Why couldn't I remember my own phone number?

I can, I told myself. It's 555–1314.

I glanced down at the phone. There was a phone number printed on a little label: 555–1314.

Why did I know Penelope's number and not my own?

The same way I knew where Tiffany lived and how to drive her car.

I began to feel sick.

Something strange was happening and I couldn't stop shaking as I thought about the consequences of this wish.

I looked around for a phone book. There wasn't any. There was a little address book in the desk drawer, but my number wouldn't be in Penelope's address book.

Information! I'll call the operator and get the number.
I dialed 411.

"May I help you?"

"Yes. The number for Edgar Warren," I whispered.

"I can't hear you."

"Edgar Warren." I hoped Mr. Kellogg was asleep. I hoped my real father wasn't asleep. I hoped I still had a real father.

"Do you have an address on that?" the operator asked.

"Sure, it's—"

I couldn't remember my address. For a moment I thought I was going to pass out. Then my voice started to recite an address before I realized I was saying it. "Forty-four-sixty-three Albermarle Avenue. Apartment three-G."

That wasn't my address. I mean, the Warrens' address. We lived in a house, not an apartment.

I looked down at Penelope's address book. On the first page Penelope had printed her name and address: Penelope Kellogg, 4463 Albermarle Avenue, apartment 3G.

I dropped the phone.

It looked as if I would be Penelope Kellogg for life. I had her hair, her eyes, her boyfriend, and her phone number.

It would be only a matter of time till my memories of my old self and my former family disappeared. They would fade as they had when I was Tiffany.

Not only that—what if there was no Edgar Warren anymore? Maybe if I was Penelope now, I never was Jean.

And if I never was Jean, maybe there wasn't any

Edgar Warren. Or any Leona Warren. And no Richie Warren.

I must admit that I was not as alarmed at the prospect of being an only child as I was at my parents' possible predicament.

I didn't have the courage to call Information again to see if my family existed. I couldn't bear to know the worst right now.

I'd get through tonight somehow. But I wouldn't sleep. If I fell asleep I might wake up without remembering anything about my real family.

I switched on the pink TV. I kept the volume very low so I wouldn't disturb Mr. Kellogg.

I heard the familiar music before the picture appeared. And the announcer's voice: ". . . somewhere beyond reality . . . in the Twilight Zone. . . ."

"Yeah, right." I pushed the switch off. There was nothing TV could tell me now about the Twilight Zone.

The book on the desk was a dictionary. I found a pen in the top desk drawer.

I'd play the dictionary game.

I let the book fall open and closed my eyes. I circled the pen over the dictionary and brought it down onto the page.

I opened my eyes. "Puparium: the outer shell formed from the larval skin that covers a coarctate pupa."

Swell. Really useful word. I didn't even know what a coarctate pupa was, let alone its larval skin.

Ordinarily I would look up all the words in the definition I didn't understand. But I wasn't in the mood to learn new words. Tonight I wanted to play the game to find out my fate.

I remembered the beautiful unabridged dictionary that my parents gave me for my birthday. I remembered playing the game with it for the first time.

I even remembered the words I'd picked. Man and snuggle.

I couldn't snuggle with Mr. Kellogg, but he was a man. I'd snuggled twice with Ned Bayer. The dictionary fortune had been pretty accurate.

I needed a book. A big book. Something to read for the next seven hours. I opened the bedroom door and looked down the hall. The lights in the living room were out and the door opposite my room was closed.

I crept down the hall to the living room. I told myself I was being silly to worry that Mr. Kellogg would catch me. He was an English teacher. He wouldn't be surprised to find his daughter reading a good book.

I found a floor lamp in the living room by bumping into it. I turned it on and began to examine the books in the floor-to-ceiling shelves.

I let my eyes roam around the titles till I found the fiction section. I had read some of the books, but I'd never heard of a lot of the others.

I was surprised to find a whole row of Heartthrob High paperbacks. I couldn't imagine why Mr. Kellogg had them in his bookcase. He couldn't be reading them.

I read the whole series when I was ten. They were all about identical triplets named Chastity, BonBon and Fleur. The biggest problem they ever faced was when

BonBon lost her lipstick right before their audition for a TV commercial.

I supposed they were Penelope's books. Maybe she'd grown out of them too.

Finally I picked out the thickest book I could find. *War and Peace,* by Tolstoy.

I'd heard of it, but I'd never read it. It was so heavy that I had to hold it with both hands as I carried it to a chair. It would get me through the night.

It would get me through March and April, if I needed to stay awake that long.

I sat down next to the lamp, put my feet up on a footstool, and began to read *War and Peace.*

Twelve

When I opened my eyes, sun was streaming in through the living room windows and Mr. Kellogg was hovering over me looking anxious.

"What are you doing in here?" he asked. "Didn't you get any sleep?"

"I must have." I felt fuzzy. "I just woke up."

"Is that *War and Peace*?" he asked.

"Yes."

He stared at me. "Are you positive you didn't sustain a concussion?"

"Sure I'm positive." As positive as I was about being Jean Warren, even if I couldn't remember my address or telephone number. I was relieved that I didn't seem to have lost any more of my memory, even though I'd fallen asleep.

"Penelope, this is wonderful! I'm so proud of you. This is the happiest day of my life."

"Why?" I asked.

"Well, honey, you never read anything except those Heartthrob High books. Naturally I was disappointed that you didn't inherit my love of good literature."

I should have guessed that the person who lived with fuchsia, French provincial, and ruffles wouldn't progress past Heartthrob High in her reading.

"Well, I guess I'm turning over a new leaf," I said. "Ha-ha. Joke. Get it? New page, new leaf?"

Daddy smiled delightedly. "I get it. I just can't believe you thought it up."

If I ever got out of this wish, and if Mr. Kellogg really had a daughter named Penelope, it was going to be a big letdown for him when she was restored to her rightful father.

"I guess I'd better get dressed for school," I said. I looked down at my lap. *War and Peace* covered more of it than the pink skirt did.

"It's Sunday," said Mr. Kellogg.

"Oh, right. Um—what's the date?"

"February fifteenth."

"What year?"

"I'm calling the doctor," he said. "You're just not yourself."

Suddenly there was a short, sharp ring.

"Telephone," I said.

"Doorbell," he said. He cocked his head to one side and looked at me, worried.

He opened the door.

Ned stood in the doorway.

I felt suddenly giddy.

100

"Are you feeling better, Penelope?" he asked. He sounded cool and formal.

"Fine," I said.

"I'd like to speak to you." He turned to Mr. Kellogg. "Would it be all right to take Penelope out to breakfast?"

"That would be great," I said.

Mr. Kellogg frowned. "I was about to call the doctor."

"Oh, Daddy, I don't need a doctor. I'm bursting with health."

I planned it all in an instant. Ned would spend an hour or so kissing me and telling me how much he loved me, and then he'd drive me to Jean Warren's house so I could get the lamp and be myself again. I didn't know what would happen after that, but the vital thing was to get the lamp.

I grabbed Ned's arm. "Let's go!"

"Your coat," Daddy said. He reached into a closet and pulled out a purple leather jacket.

"Don't be too long," he said.

I put on the jacket and caught a glimpse of myself in the mirror inside the closet door. The chartreuse camisole, the barely visible pink skirt—I wouldn't be caught dead in that outfit. But I was Penelope. As soon as I was Jean again I'd be wearing my own clothes.

I wiggled my fingers good-bye at Mr. Kellogg and nearly dragged Ned out of the apartment.

"What's going on?" he said. "You're still acting weird."

"I'm not myself."

"You weren't yourself last night, either," he said. "When do you plan on being yourself again?"

"Any minute now." I giggled.

"Penelope, this isn't a joke. You were pretty cold to me last night."

I wondered how warm he expected me to be. Did we have a special tree in this wish too?

He opened a door with an exit sign above it. I followed him down two flights of stairs.

He shoved open another door and led me out into the parking lot.

"Where's your car?" I asked.

He stopped to squint at me. "Your father's right," he said. "You do need a doctor."

"No, really," I said. "There's a reasonable explanation." I thought about that for a moment. "Well, maybe reasonable isn't exactly the right word."

In a flash my mind was made up. I had to tell Ned the truth. I needed his help. I only hoped that he wouldn't agree with Daddy that I was a severe nut case.

"You're not going to plead temporary insanity, are you?" He must have been reading my mind. I followed him to a gleaming black Corvette and got in when he opened the door for me. "How could you forget a Corvette?"

He slid into the driver's seat and slammed his door shut.

I took a deep breath. "Ned," I began, "you're not going to believe this, but . . ."

*   *   *

"You're right," he said. "I don't believe it. How could you have made up a story like that?"

"I couldn't."

"This is crazy," he said.

"Let's not use that word," I said. "Let's call the whole thing unusual. You can help me prove it's true. You're my only hope."

I looked into his beautiful, troubled eyes and waited for his answer.

"Why didn't you tell your father about this?"

"Because he wouldn't believe me. He already thinks I'm crazy because I was reading *War and Peace*."

Ned looked startled. "He could be right," he said.

"If you'll take me to Jean Warren's house I'll prove I'm not crazy."

"Okay, okay," he said. "I'll take you. But it's hard to believe you have such a vivid imagination."

"I don't. My mother says I have no imagination at all."

"Your mother?"

"Well, Mrs. Warren, if you want to get technical."

He started the car.

"We're going to need a phone book," I said.

"You mean, you don't know your own address?"

"It's not my address anymore. That's why we have to go there."

"I know the address," Ned said.

"You do?" I threw my arms around his neck and nearly choked him. "I'm real! Jean is real. And you're real! I told you."

"It doesn't prove anything," he said. He backed out of the parking space and headed for the street.

"How do you know where Jean Warren lives?" I asked.

"You're trying to make me forget about last night," he said. "But you can't put me off forever. Once this nonsense is over you're going to have some explaining to do."

"I will," I said. "I promise." I couldn't tell him that once "this nonsense" was over I wouldn't be around to explain anything.

I recognized our street immediately. I knew my house was the gray-and-white one before Ned pulled into the driveway.

My heart began to pound wildly.

If everything worked out right, I was about to come face-to-face with myself.

Richie opened the door.

"Who are you?" Rude as always. My brother certainly hadn't changed.

"Friends of Jean's," I said.

"She doesn't have any friends."

"Will you stop saying that?" I cried.

"Is she home?" Ned asked.

"Yeah." He turned and yelled up the stairs. "JEAN!"

I could feel Ned's eyes on me. I thought he must be trying to decide whether I was crazy or not.

Richie lost interest. He wandered off toward the den.

"Let's go in," I said.

"Do you think we should?"

"Trust me, Ned. I live here."

My father came to the door. He looked wonderful. I wanted to throw my arms around him.

"Hi," he said. "Something we can do for you?"

Ned shot me a withering glare. "You live here?" he muttered.

"We came to see Jean," I said.

"That's nice." I could see he was happy that Jean was having friends visit. "She's in her room. I'll get her."

"That's okay," I said. "I know the way."

"You do?" he looked puzzled.

But I was already halfway up the first flight of stairs.

I was surprised that my legs could carry me up the second flight. I was weak and scared and my palms were so damp that my hand kept sliding on the banister.

Ned followed me.

The door to my room was open. I held my breath for a long moment. I was afraid to look inside. I didn't know whether it would be worse to see myself, or to not see myself.

"Well?" Ned gestured toward the door.

"I'm scared," I whispered. "This is the most frightening moment of my life. What if I'm not there?"

He put his hand on my shoulder. "If you're not there we'll go back to your house and call the doctor for you."

"But what if I *am* there?"

"Then I'll go back to my house and call the doctor for me."

I giggled a little, in spite of the fact that goose bumps were forming all over my entire body.

"You go first," I said.

He tapped on the open door and walked into the room.

"Hi," he said.

"Ned Bayer!" my voice replied. "What are you doing here?"

Thirteen

I nearly fell through the doorway of my room. Sitting at the desk, arm on the unabridged dictionary, was me. I ordered myself to keep breathing.

I stared at me—I mean, Jean Warren—and she—I mean, I—stared back. I was kind of surprised to see that I—that is, Jeannie—wasn't bad-looking. Actually she/I was kind of pretty.

She had long, smooth, light brown hair with golden highlights. Her (my?) eyes were green with little flashes of gold in them. Did I really look like that?

"Do you two know each other?" asked Ned.

"No," said Jean.

"Yes," I said. The lamp. If I could just light the lamp.

I looked around the room. The last time I had used it, it had been on the desk.

"It's not here!" I cried. "Ned, the lamp isn't here!"

He wasn't paying much attention to me. He was gazing at Jean Warren.

"I didn't really expect it to be," he said.

"What if there is no lamp?" I said. "Maybe in this wish I didn't get a magic lantern!"

"A magic lantern," Jean said. "That's odd."

"What's odd?" Ned couldn't take his eyes off Jean.

"Just that my aunt and uncle gave me a lamp that sort of looked like a magic lantern for my birthday. Last May. How did you know about it?"

"Where is it? It's very important. Honestly, if I could just see it—"

"I took it back to the store," she said calmly. She pointed to an ancient-looking book on the night table. "I got an early edition of *Huckleberry Finn* instead. What do I need with a lamp?"

"Noo!" I wailed. "What store?"

"Unique Antiques," Jean said. "You sure are getting hysterical about a moldy old lamp."

"It's February now?" I asked Ned.

He nodded.

"Then that lamp was returned nine and a half months ago," I figured. "Or—" I held my head. "Or two and a half months from now."

"What?" said Jean.

"Whichever it was, it'll be gone by this time." I sat on the edge of Jean's bed. It wasn't my bed anymore. It might never be my bed again.

"I know it's gone," Jean said. "My aunt and uncle bought it again. It was pretty embarrassing."

"You mean, Aunt Jean and Uncle Rocky *have* it?"

Ned and Jean managed to stop gazing at each other for a moment. They both looked at me questioningly.

108

"You know my aunt and uncle?" Jean asked.

"Could you ask them to give you back the lamp?" I said.

"Are you kidding? I've already had enough problems with that thing."

"What do you mean?" asked Ned.

"I returned it without telling anyone," said Jean. "My aunt went into the store and thought the lamp was a match for the one they gave me. So she bought it, and then found out it was the same lamp. It was very embarrassing."

"I know just how you feel," I said, "believe me I do. But this is a matter of life and death."

"Aren't you being a little melodramatic?" Jean said.

"I'm not being melodramatic enough!"

Ned looked at Jean and shrugged. "I could drive you to your aunt's house if she doesn't live too far away."

"She doesn't." Jean and I said it simultaneously.

"How did you know?" Jean asked me.

"I'll explain it to you on the way to Aunt Jean's." I hugged Ned. It might be the last chance I ever had. "You're a lifesaver," I told him.

"What will I tell them?" asked Jean as Ned started the car.

"You could tell them that you have a buyer for the lamp who's willing to pay a lot of money for it," I suggested.

"They'll think I want it back only because it turned out to be valuable."

"What's wrong with that?" I said. "It's a perfectly logical reason."

"Not if it's really a magic lamp," Jean said.

"Good grief, you're right," I said. "What if Arthur is Aunt Jean's genie now?"

Jean laughed. "I was only kidding. You have some imagination. This is the most unbelievable story I've ever heard—after the one about the Tooth Fairy."

"But that's just it," I said. "I don't have any imagination at all. I'm just like you. In fact, I *am* you."

"That's impossible," Jean said. "Take the parkway east till you get to exit thirty," she told Ned.

"I knew that!" I said.

"Sure." Jean sounded sarcastic.

We turned onto the ramp leading to the parkway.

"When you get off at exit thirty," I said, "turn left at the end of the street, then left again till you get to Potter's Lane."

Jean leaned forward over the front seat. "How did you know that?"

"I'm you," I said.

She sat back. For a moment she didn't say anything.

"You can't be me," she said softly. "Or you wouldn't be wearing that outfit. I don't have any clothes like that."

"I know you don't," I agreed. "I mean, we don't. I'm only Penelope Kellogg on the outside. Inside I'm really you. I mean, us."

"Penelope Kellogg?" Jean shrieked. "You're Mr. Kellogg's wife?"

"His daughter," I said. "His wife's dead."

110

"Oh, good," said Jean. She sounded relieved.

Ned looked even more puzzled than he had before, but I knew why she was glad to find out Mr. Kellogg had no wife.

Maybe in real life he did. Maybe his wife was dead just for this wish, and when—if—I could get things back to normal, he'd be married.

But I suspected I wouldn't care if he was married or not. After this I'd never be able to think of Mr. Kellogg as anyone but Daddy.

"Exit thirty," Ned said.

"It's about four minutes to Aunt Jean's," I said, "if you make the light at the end of Potter's Lane."

"That's right," Jean said. "This is scary."

"You think that's scary?" I said. "You should be in my position."

And suddenly she was.

I mean, I was.

That is, Jean was.

It's impossible to describe what happened, because I really don't know what happened, except that in a flash I was in the backseat, and Penelope Kellogg was sitting next to Ned in the front seat. She was wearing the purple leather jacket and craning her neck to look at me.

"I don't believe this."

"I know you don't," said the girl in the front seat. "We'll be at Aunt Jean's in a minute, and you'll see for yourself."

"This can't be happening," I said. "I mean, right now. How can we both be me? That's against the laws of physics, or something."

"There's the house," Penelope said. She pointed to a white brick ranch house in the middle of the block.

"That's right," I said. "But how did you know that? And how did I know you knew that?"

"Forget it," said Penelope. "You can't figure out magic."

Ned drove the Corvette into the driveway in front of the garage.

"But I don't believe in magic," I said. "I never did."

"Neither did I," said Penelope. "But trust me on this one."

Uncle Rocky answered the door. Aunt Jean wasn't home, and I thought that was a good sign. I told Uncle Rocky that Penelope and Ned wanted to see the lamp because they might be able to use it as a prop in a school play.

Penelope looked impressed at the lie. Ned nodded and gave me a little secret smile.

Uncle Rocky showed us into the living room. The lamp was on a small antique desk, next to an inkwell and pen stand.

"Thank goodness," Penelope said.

"Must be a really important play you're putting on," said Uncle Rocky.

"It is," Penelope said. "And you're so sweet to let us use the lamp."

"Well, sure, why not?" Uncle Rocky looked flattered.

Ned winked at me.

Suddenly I felt an awful, hollow coldness in the pit of my stomach. I didn't know what was going to happen next, but I knew that Ned might never kiss me again.

Penelope was going to wish to be me. And then what would happen to me? What would happen to all of us?

"Anyone have a match?" Penelope asked.

Uncle Rocky handed her a lighter.

"Good," she said. "This is easier than doing it with a match. Here we go." She clicked the Bic and brought the lighter down inside the lamp.

"Wait!" I said. I kissed Ned on the lips. It might be my last chance to do it ever again.

!

I was standing near the desk in my room. The lamp was right there in front of me. So was Arthur. He was sitting cross-legged on my dresser, checking himself out in the mirror.

"You think I should trim this?" he asked, fingering his moustache.

I tried not to scream.

"Arthur," I said. "I am not the person to ask about cutting your moustache. If I were you I wouldn't let me anywhere near you with a sharp pair of scissors."

Arthur sighed deeply. "What is it this time?" he asked. "Didn't this one work out either?"

I nearly did scream. "No, this one didn't work out either! You made Mr. Kellogg my *father,* for Pete's sake."

He reached into a pocket of his harem pants and pulled out a piece of blue paper. He held it up for me to see.

"Just in case," he said, "I thought I'd keep a copy of your original wish. This is exactly what you said."

I looked at the paper. Written in curvy, elegant script was, "I wish Mr. Kellogg—Mr. Gerald Kellogg, my English teacher—loved me. I wish he were holding me in his arms right this minute."

"Oh, no!" I groaned. "How could I have been so stupid?"

"Beats me." Arthur folded up the blue paper and stuck it back in his pocket.

"I still wasn't specific enough!"

"Now you're catching on," he said. "Want to try another wish?"

"Not yet. It's going to take me a while to get over this one."

"It would be much easier if you'd wish for money," he said. "Money is a snap."

"Yeah, well, maybe I will next time."

I felt awfully depressed. For a while, even though I was Mr. Kellogg's daughter and had a fuchsia room, at least I had Ned. Now I didn't have Ned and I certainly didn't want Mr. Kellogg anymore.

That's when I decided to write all of this down.

I didn't expect anyone to believe it. I just wanted to get the facts straight before my memory of the events started to fade. I thought that making a written record might help me to understand some of what happened.

It took me two weeks of writing to get it all down. I did my homework every night before dinner, and then afterward I would write until midnight. I got writer's cramp every night but I didn't ask Arthur to cure it. In fact, for those two weeks I didn't ask Arthur for anything, except an occasional midnight snack.

By the time I finished my story he was pretty bored. "You're not giving me any exercise," he complained. "Conjuring up a pizza is not much of a challenge. I'm getting flabby."

"Well, I'm done," I said, putting down my pen. "But if you can't help me figure this out, I'll have to try and analyze it myself. There has to be some logic to the wishing process. There has to be an explanation of why every wish went wrong."

"Why?" he asked.

"Because nothing happens without a cause. And everything that happens has an effect."

"Even magic?" he said.

"Of course. That's why I'm afraid to try any more wishes before I know the rules."

"I told you the rules," he said.

"I don't think you told me all of them."

"Don't you want money?" Arthur asked. "Or fame?"

"If I asked you to make me rich and famous you'd probably turn me into a notorious bank robber."

Arthur nodded. "That would be one way to grant your wish."

"You see, Arthur, that's just what I mean. I'm reading over all these wishes I made and trying to figure out why every single one of them got screwed up."

"Well, don't look at me," said Arthur. "I answer wishes, not questions."

In school I discovered that my crush on Mr. Kellogg had really disappeared. Which was just as well, since he mentioned in class one day that it was his wife's birthday. He didn't say anything about a daughter.

But I blushed every time I passed Ned Bayer in the halls.

Even though he didn't know that we had done some major-league kissing while I was Penelope Kellogg and Tiffany Tupperman, I had a crazy feeling that he knew what I was thinking when I looked at him.

I'd never said three words to Ned Bayer in my whole life. At least, before I got the lamp. If I didn't blush and trip every time I ran into him, he wouldn't know I was alive.

Lynn said that he and Tiffany were definitely broken up. I still couldn't figure out why. He was mad at Tiffany when I was Tiffany, but the Cloud of Mystification should have made them both forget what happened during my wish.

Why hadn't their relationship gone back to normal when Tiffany was herself again?

Talking to Arthur was getting me nowhere. And if I tried to discuss this with Lynn, she wouldn't believe me and we'd probably end up on *Name That Poison* again. And after that, the Cloud of Mystification would erase her memories of Arthur and the lamp, and I'd be right back where I started.

"Look," said Arthur one afternoon, "this is getting ridiculous. You have all my mystical powers at your fingertips and you're using me as a delivery boy. Here's your Big Mac."

"Thank you," I said.

"You're going to be sorry you didn't use me better after I'm gone," he said.

"I know, I know."

"In fact, if you don't make some decent wishes I might not be able to stay here. I'm wasted on you."

"But I'm scared," I said. "I forgot to take the lamp with me last time and look what happened. I could get into another terrible wish and never be able to get out."

"I'll remind you to take the lamp," he said. "I won't grant the wish until you're holding the lamp."

"You're sure that will work?" I knew I was frittering away the chances of a lifetime, but it was frightening to consider what my lifetime would be if I could never get back to myself again.

"It should work," Arthur said.

"What do you mean, should?"

"Listen, life doesn't come with a guarantee," he said. "Neither does magic. You have to take your chances."

"Good point," I admitted.

"What good is staying alone in your room?" he asked. "Come hear the music play."

"That sounds familiar."

"Does it? I thought I made it up." He rubbed his blue hands together. "Okey dokey, what'll it be? Queen of England? President of the United States? Movie star?"

"You know that I've been writing about my adventures," I began.

"I wouldn't call your wishes very adventurous," he

snorted. "After Alexander the Great and Napoleon you're a distinct letdown."

"I'm sorry. Anyway, I think what I've written is pretty good. I mean, I could never dream up a story like this, but I think I have a knack for writing."

"You want to be another Shakespeare! Terrific. Let's get started."

"Wait!" I yelled. I grabbed the lamp. "I don't want to be another Shakespeare. I want to be a modern, best-selling author, and do book tours and stuff like that. And I want to live in a posh penthouse apartment."

Arthur looked excited. "Famous, check. Modern, check. Book tours, check. Penthouse, check. I think I've got it."

"I hope so," I said nervously.

"Ready?" he asked.

"I hope so."

"Okey dokey."

!

Fourteen

I was seated at a table equipped with two micro-
phones. One mike was in front of me. I guessed I was in a
radio station being interviewed. Behind the other microphone a sour-faced man with little slits for eyes glared at
me.

I wondered what book I was promoting. I figured it
was my newest best seller, but I had no idea what I had
written.

It would be all right, though. When I was Tiffany I
knew how to drive a car, so I assumed I'd have all the
information I'd need for the interview.

"What do you say, Jillian Farquahar, to those parents
and teachers who denounce your books as shallow and
materialistic—"

Who was Jillian Farquahar?

"—and that your heroines, Chastity, BonBon, and Fleur,
are terrible role models for contemporary young women?"

"But I'm not—" I stopped myself. I must be. Suddenly I remembered who Jillian Farquahar was. Arthur had turned me into the author of the Heartthrob High books.

The nasty-looking man thrust his chin out as if he were daring me to punch him.

But this time I had the lamp with me. It was on the table right next to my microphone, so I could vamoose if things got too unpleasant.

Not that they were pleasant right now. Arthur was going to have some more explaining to do.

"I see you won't answer my questions," the man snarled.

"I didn't say—"

He interrupted me. "Have you the intestinal fortitude to take phone calls from our listeners? They won't be as gentle with their comments as I am."

"How could they be worse?" I said. It might be interesting to be controversial. And escape was only a wish away.

Lights started to flash on a panel in front of us.

"Here's our first caller." The man punched a button and I could hear a woman's voice coming over the phone.

"My daughter read one of your books and now she wants to be a cheerleader for the Dallas Cowboys when she grows up."

"That's not my fault," I said.

"You mean that you refuse to take responsibility for the warped values you proclaim in your stories?" The man curled his lip in a sneer.

"This isn't much fun," I said.

120

"We didn't invite you to sit in The Hot Seat for fun."

I heard a click and then another voice over the phone. This time it sounded like a young girl. "My mom won't let me read your books anymore," she said. "And I really like your books."

"Thank you," I said.

"Especially the sexy parts."

I gasped. "There aren't any sexy parts in the Heartthrob High books."

"Do you mean to tell us," the host demanded, "that you don't call those shameful scenes sexy? You believe they're suitable for teenagers? You think it's okay to write *smut* for the children of this country?"

"It isn't Heartthrob High," the caller said. "It's Heartbreak High. Gee, you ought to know the name of your own series."

"I do," I said. "It's Heartthrob."

"No it's not," the girl insisted. "I had the whole series until my mother made me throw them out. It's Heartbreak High."

"Let me get this straight," the host said. "You deny your involvement in this sickening spectacle of corruption and vice that you created in order to weaken the moral fiber of American teenagers?"

"No!"

"Then you don't deny it?"

I held my head in my hands. "Arthur's done it again."

"You have an accomplice in this business?" the man asked. "A collaborator named Arthur?"

121

I picked up the lamp. For a moment I entertained the idea of barbecuing Arthur.

"I wish this interview were over," I said, "and that I were in my posh penthouse apartment overlooking Central Park."

!

A uniformed man held the lobby door open for me and tipped his hat.

"Good evening, Ms. Farquahar. I'm sorry about the elevator."

The lobby was fantastic. Rose carpeting, soft lighting, a small fountain, and some green plants in the center. Talk about posh! This place was dripping with posh.

I tucked the lamp under my arm. I had a portfolio under my other arm. I assumed that my latest manuscript was in the portfolio.

This was going to be good.

"Why are you sorry about the elevator?" I asked.

"They haven't fixed it yet. You'll have to walk upstairs again, I'm afraid."

"Walk? Upstairs? Again?"

He nodded sympathetically. "I'm afraid so. All twenty-nine floors."

"I'm definitely going to barbecue Arthur," I said.

"I beg your pardon, Ms. Farquahar?"

"Never mind," I said. "I'm learning how to deal with these little glitches." I tapped on the lamp. "I wish the elevator would work so it can take me up to my posh penthouse apartment on the twenty-ninth floor."

!

"Here you are, Miss. The penthouse." The elevator man slid the door open and tipped his cap. I stepped out of the elevator and right into the entry hall of my apartment.

"Now, this is more like it," I said. From the hall I could see the living room windows, which spanned most of one wall. It was dark, and the lights of New York glittered like diamonds on black velvet.

I walked toward the windows, almost hypnotized by the beauty of the nightscape.

The living room was huge. All the furniture was white. The rugs were white. There was even a grand piano in gleaming white wood.

Everything was modern and immaculate. It all looked brand-new. It was apparent that my brother Richie wasn't in this wish.

I went from the living room down another hallway where I thought the bedrooms ought to be. One of the bedrooms was obviously my writing room.

There was a computer, a printer, and two big type-writers. Along one wall was a couch with velvet throw pillows. On the wall above the couch were covers from the Heartthrob High series. They were all framed.

"I sure wrote a lot of books," I said to myself. "I must be making a bundle." I put the lamp and my portfolio down on a desk. I knelt on the couch to get a close-up look at the covers. Heartbreak High, by Jillian Farquahar. No! That's wrong!

I sighed. There seemed to be no limit to Arthur's talent for screwing up. But I was famous and I was rich and I was a best-selling author, so how much could I complain? After all, Arthur only missed by one syllable this time.

I glanced at the desk, where I had put down my portfolio and the lamp. A piece of newspaper was on top of my portfolio.

I picked up the paper. It was a newspaper article. The headline read, *"CALIFORNIA EDUCATION OFFICIALS BAN BOOKS BY POPULAR AUTHOR."*

Officials from the Department of Education for the state of California have declared that all books by best-selling author Jillian Farquahar be removed from the shelves of all schools and public libraries.

Some community leaders are also preparing a campaign to prohibit stores in their districts from selling Farquahar's megahit series, Heartbreak High.

When reached for comment on this ruling, Ms. Farquahar responded, "Who cares? I've already made a bundle on those books."

I sat down at the desk, ready to burst into tears. I felt awful. Here I was, a famous author, but I was famous for the wrong reasons. People hated me. A whole state hated me.

If I was the kind of writer who said, "Who cares? I've already made a bundle," it was no wonder.

There's no need to panic, I told myself. It's very simple. I'll just make a wish to adjust this wish, the way I did with the elevator. This is a neat apartment and I'm sure I'll enjoy being filthy rich. All I have to do is to wish to be a *beloved* best-selling author.

I pulled the lid off the lamp. A curl of smoke rose from it. The candle was still burning.

"I wish I were a *well-liked,* famous, best-selling, rich, modern author," I said.

!

I looked around. Everything seemed the same. That was fine. It was supposed to be the same, except for the kind of writer I was.

But considering Arthur's track record, I was sure there had to be a catch somewhere. I checked my arms and legs. They were all there where they should be, and none of them were in casts.

I walked back into the living room.

It was exactly the same. Except for the five small children finger-painting on the rug.

"Yikes!"

The five children looked up as I yiked. They were all younger than Richie. Their little faces glowed with love. Also with chocolate and finger paint.

"Mommy, Mommy!" they shrieked. They jumped up and charged at me.

"Can I have a—"

"Cookie!"

"Apple!"

"Bath!"

"Ice cream!"

"German shepherd!"

"HELP!" I yelled.

They flung themselves at me and grabbed onto my legs, arms, sleeves, and belt.

They were dirty and sticky and very badly behaved. No wonder they loved me. Obviously I let them do whatever they wanted. The living room was a disgusting mess. All the white furniture was gouged and stained and grimy. Someone had colored on the lid of the white piano.

"MOMMY! MOMMY! MOMMY! MOMMY! MOMMY!"

"This was not what I meant," I screamed, "by well-liked!"

With kids clinging to my body I hauled myself and my—blecchh—family back into my writing room.

The lamp was still on the desk. I realized that I was lucky. I had forgotten to hold onto it when I revised the wish.

The candle was still lit. A small puff of smoke hovered over it.

"Come on out, Arthur," I ordered. "You can run but you can't hide."

When all of Arthur emerged from the lamp, he sat cross-legged in the air, frowning and riffling through a batch of papers.

"How did it go this time?" he asked, looking up from the papers.

"You don't know?" I said. "You really aren't lousing things up on purpose?"

"Certainly not!" Arthur looked down at the papers again. "You are Jean Roxbury, aren't you?"

"I'm Jean Warren!"

"I don't suppose Roxbury could be your married name?" he asked.

"I'm only fifteen!" I said. "Jean Roxbury is my *aunt!*"

"Oops," said Arthur.

Fifteen

Before you could say "Okey dokey" I was childless again and back in my own room. The lamp was on my desk and so was Arthur. He was still holding the sheaf of papers. He frowned and scratched his head.

"What did 'oops' mean?" I demanded.

"I think I've figured out why your wishes aren't coming true the way you want them to." He cleared his throat and shuffled the papers around. He wouldn't look me in the eye.

"Why?" My voice sounded so menacing that I hardly recognized myself. "Why does everything I wish for get loused up?"

Arthur hesitated. He looked at the lamp as if he were tempted to dive into it and disappear.

"You're going to be mad," he warned.

"It wasn't my fault at all, was it?" I asked.

"Well, no," Arthur admitted.

"It had nothing to do with my being a poor wisher, did it?"

"No," said Arthur. He stood up and poised one blue toe over the edge of the lamp. He was preparing for a quick getaway.

"This is really sort of amusing, if you keep things in perspective." He was stalling.

"I'm not going to be amused, am I?" I said.

"Look at it this way," he coaxed. "You've still got your health."

"You were supposed to be my Aunt Jean's genie, weren't you?" I asked. "I got the wrong genie. I mean, you got the wrong Jeannie."

"I don't know how this could have happened," he said. "All right, a couple of hundred years ago I made one tiny mistake and mixed up Benjamin Franklin and Benedict Arnold, but I never granted wishes to a minor before."

"What difference does my age make?" I asked.

"You're only fifteen," he said. "You're too young to have a genie. Having a genie requires stability and maturity and control over your emotions."

"You did my homework!" I screamed. "How old did you think I was?"

"See," Arthur said. "You're losing control again."

He folded up the batch of papers and stuffed it into the breast pocket in his vest. "I'm going to have to check the records some more," he said. "It may take me a little while."

He began to whirl around over the lamp.

"No, wait!" I said. "Don't go yet. I have to ask you—"

But Arthur dove headfirst into the lamp.

The candle went out.

I found matches in the desk drawer and lit the lamp again.

Nothing in my life had prepared me for the emptiness I felt now that Arthur was gone. Because Arthur was definitely gone. The candle burned brightly, but that's all that happened.

I felt even worse than I did when I had to give up Ned.

But maybe Arthur wasn't gone forever. He'd said that checking up on his mistake might take a little while. He didn't say he had to leave forever.

Of course, in Arthur's terms a little while could mean a hundred years. And even if he came back tomorrow he wouldn't be my genie anymore.

Without Arthur I felt lonelier and more friendless than I ever had before. I really didn't have anyone to talk to except Lynn. And she was already in the dance club and friendly with the most popular girl in school. She wouldn't have a whole lot of time for me anymore.

I didn't confide in my parents, but what was there to confide? They already knew I was no Tiffany Tupperman, and I knew that my solitary habits worried them. I didn't want to make them feel worse by telling them how badly I felt.

My brother hated me, but who wanted to talk to Richie?

Arthur had loused up all my wishes, but at least there were people in them. People who cared about me, people who loved me—even if one turned out to be my father.

If only I had one more wish. Maybe it wouldn't work, but this time I would wish only to be happy. It wasn't very specific, but I didn't care how I was happy, and what I was happy doing, as long as I was happy.

I watched the candle burn for a moment and wondered where Arthur was when I didn't see him inside the lamp. And suddenly I thought that I might very well see Arthur again.

I blew out the candle, picked up the lamp, and dashed downstairs.

Riding the bus to Aunt Jean's took longer than the trip in Ned's car, but my parents were both still at work and Aunt Jean doesn't drive.

I tried to concentrate on how I would break the news of the magic lamp to her. I rehearsed several scenarios, but they all ended with Aunt Jean feeling my forehead and calling an ambulance.

I still hadn't figured out a good way to tell her about Arthur when I got off the bus. It really didn't matter what I told her, I decided. Once she lit the lamp she'd see for herself.

I ran the two blocks to Aunt Jean's house.

"This is a nice surprise," she said when she opened the door. "But shouldn't you be in school?"

"Yes, but I have to tell you something."

Aunt Jean shaded her eyes from the sunlight. I followed her into the house.

"Are you sick?" I asked her.

"Just a headache," she said. "Tension."

We went into the kitchen. She took milk and chocolate cake from the refrigerator.

"You've brought the lamp. Is it broken?"

"Not exactly. It's just sort of misplaced."

"What do you mean?"

"Do you remember my birthday when you said the lamp wasn't magic because you'd rubbed it and nothing happened?"

"Yes," she said. "It was just a joke."

"Did you ever light it?" I asked.

"No. The wick of the candle looked new so I didn't want to burn it before I gave it to you. What's all this about?"

"Would you try lighting it now?" I asked.

"But why?"

"*Please,*" I begged. "Just light the candle and you'll see why."

"All right, honey, don't get yourself so worked up." She rummaged in a drawer and pulled out a box of kitchen matches.

She struck one on the side of the box and poked it down into the lamp. "It's hard to light," she said. "Ah, there we go."

"Watch what happens," I said. I sounded confident but I wasn't at all sure that Arthur would show up. He could be anywhere by this time. If he had finished double-checking his assignment, he ought to appear now for Aunt Jean. But as a genie, Arthur was no rocket scientist.

133

Aunt Jean smiled. "If a genie comes out of that lamp I want it back."

"Yes, well, that's the whole idea."

"Jeannie, this is sil—"

"Look!" I pointed to a wisp of blue smoke rising from the candle. "Come out, Arthur!"

"Who's Arthur? Jeannie, what's the matter with you? You're acting so—"

The blue smoke swirled slowly around the room and finally collected halfway between the lamp and the ceiling. It grew larger and larger. Then it began to form the figure that I knew so well.

I looked at Aunt Jean. Her hand was pressed against her heart. Her mouth was open in an O of surprise.

"Jeannie!" She gasped. *"Jeannie!"*

"Yes, I am," said Arthur, "but I'm going to have to check your I.D." He was holding a clipboard and a quill pen. A fresh cigar was in his mouth.

"Am I glad to see you," I told him. "Even though I ought to be angry at you."

Aunt Jean whimpered and sagged against the refrigerator.

"Don't be afraid," I said. I put my arm around her. "There's nothing to be afraid of. This is Arthur."

"You see it too?"

"He's real," I said.

She shook her head, hard, as if she could deny Arthur's existence. "It's some kind of trick."

"It's no trick," I said. "I wouldn't do that to you. This is a magic lamp, and Arthur is your own, personal genie. He got us Jeans mixed up."

134

"A very understandable error," Arthur said. "You are Jean Roxbury?"

Aunt Jean nodded. She hung onto the refrigerator door handle as if she'd fall down if she let go.

"In that case, I'm at your service," said Arthur. "Your wish is my command."

"I wish you'd go away," she said.

"Okey dokey."

!

"What happened?" Aunt Jean looked around the room. Arthur was gone.

"You wished he would go away," I said. "So he did. I wish you hadn't done that."

!

"This is very confusing." Arthur reappeared over the sink. "With both of you in the same room I can't tell who's wishing what."

"This cannot be happening," said Aunt Jean. "Look Jeannie— "

"Call me Arthur," Arthur said.

"I meant Jeannie my niece!" she wailed. "Whatever this is, stop it!"

"I can't stop it," I said. "Arthur is your genie. He'll do anything you ask him. He might not do it very well—"

"Are you going to keep harping on that forever?" he grumbled.

135

"Aunt Jean, just try it. Wish for something. Anything."

"Ridiculous." she said. "All right, I'll play along with your little hoax. But I don't think it's very funny."

She rubbed her forehead. "I wish my whole family were in perfect health."

!

"What kind of a wish is that?" I asked. "How can you tell if it came true?"

"Thank you for that vote of confidence," said Arthur sarcastically.

"My headache's gone." She sounded surprised.

The phone rang. She grabbed the receiver as if she'd been waiting for an urgent call.

"What happened?" she asked into the phone. "It *did*?" Her eyes opened wide. "He said what?"

She looked dazed. "Yes, it is. A miracle. I can't believe it."

She hung up the phone. "That was Rocky. He's been having terrible backaches, so last week he went to the doctor and they discovered he had a herniated disc. The doctor said he needed an operation. He went for preliminary tests today."

She kept shaking her head as she talked, as if she couldn't believe what she was saying. "The herniated disc is healed. Completely. The doctor said that in twenty-five years of practice he never saw anything like that."

Arthur shot me a smug look. He puffed on his cigar and blew out a little smoke stream of Rx's.

"That was a pretty good wish," I said. "Even though it sounded boring."

"It certainly was a good wish," Arthur said. "A lot of people don't think about their health until it's too late."

He came down a little to hover at Aunt Jean's eye level. "It will be a pleasure working with you," he said. "What would you like next? Stocks? Diamonds? Real estate? Pizza?"

"This is too much for me," Aunt Jean said. "Does your mother know about the lamp?"

"No," I said. "Nobody knows about it."

"What did you wish for?" she asked.

"Dumb things," I said. "Mostly I wished not to be me."

"Oh, honey." She put her arm around me. "That *is* dumb. I love you."

"I know," I said. "But nobody else does."

"Of course they do."

"I mean, other than you and Uncle Rocky and my folks."

Even to myself I sounded as if I was drowning in self-pity. Arthur lounged on his back in midair with one leg over his knee. He puffed out a string of smoky hearts and flowers.

"If anybody's interested," he said, "I'm still here."

Aunt Jean put her hands on her hips and stared at Arthur. "You can do *anything*?" she asked.

"Just about."

"Stick around," she ordered.

She turned back to face me. "Why doesn't anyone

love you? Just because you haven't got a boyfriend yet doesn't mean you never will."

"I have *no* friends," I said, "except for Lynn Shoemaker, and she joined a club and is making new friends and I've been in high school for almost a year and I don't know anybody."

"Why don't you join a club?" Aunt Jean suggested.

"There aren't any clubs for the things I like to do."

"Oh, come on, Jeannie. That's a lame excuse."

"Well, I can't help it. I don't know why nobody likes me."

"You can't say nobody likes you," said Aunt Jean, "when you haven't met anybody yet. Have you tried to make friends?"

"Please," I said. "I just came here to bring you your magic lamp. I really don't want a lecture on 'You have to be a friend to make a friend.' I'm shy, okay?"

"You're scared," she said.

"I know that. I just don't know how not to be scared."

"You seemed pretty brave to me," Arthur said suddenly. "You'd be amazed at how many people are terrified when I first appear. You were one of the calmest humans I've ever met."

Aunt Jean rubbed her forehead again, not as if she had a headache, but as if she was trying to figure something out. She'd drive herself nuts if she tried to figure out the rules of wishing. But maybe Arthur would be a better genie now that he was with his rightful mistress.

"I'd better go," I said. "My parents will be home soon."

"When you feel like it," Aunt Jean said, "I wish you'd talk to me."

!

The next time I looked at the clock an hour had passed and I had told Aunt Jean practically my entire autobiography for the past year. I told her almost everything that had happened, from the time I started high school in September to an hour ago, when she had wished I'd talk to her.

"I didn't realize you were so unhappy," she said.

"Sometimes I didn't realize it myself," I said.

"But you can make wishes for another person," she said thoughtfully.

Arthur yawned. "Yes. And all this activity is wearing me out."

"Don't be sarcastic," Aunt Jean said. "I'll give you plenty to keep you busy."

"I really have to get home," I said. "I'll miss you, Arthur, strange as that seems."

He stood up and stretched. "Strange as it seems," he said, "I'll miss you too."

Sixteen

"Jeannie! Dad says do you want an Egg McMuffin?" Richie burst into my room.

"Will you please knock?" I said.

He tapped his knuckles against the open door. "Knock knock," he said, "do you want an Egg McMuffin?"

"Do you ever get that feeling of *déjà vu*?" I asked him.

"Deja who?"

"Forget it. Tell him yes." I almost expected to have an Egg McMuffin materialize in my hand, but it didn't. The cushy days of instant snack deliveries were over.

Why don't I feel worse? I wondered. It had taken me a long time to get to sleep last night. I'd kept missing Arthur.

But I hopped out of bed and headed for the shower feeling positively cheerful. Even though it was a school day.

At breakfast Richie eyed me suspiciously. "What's the matter with you today?" he asked. "Why aren't you calling me names?"

"Don't look a gift horse in the mouth," my mother said.

"If she keeps scarfing down food this way she'll turn into a horse," he said.

I smiled sweetly at him and polished off a second Egg McMuffin.

"You're right," my father told Richie. "This is spooky."

"I love it," my mother said. "Jeannie, you look terrific today. Is that a new sweater?"

"Nope. Old sweater."

"I know what it is," Richie said. "She's smiling. She's got globs of egg in her teeth, but she's smiling."

"This is an unusually pleasant morning," my father said. "Don't louse it up."

I was as surprised as anyone else by this strange new mood. I realized that I was looking forward to school, that I wanted to be with people.

Today, I promised myself, when I meet Ned Bayer in the hall, I'm not going to turn red and stumble over my own feet. I'm going to say hello to him.

The phone rang.

My mother answered it. She looked surprised as she handed me the receiver. "It's Aunt Jean. She wants to talk to you."

"Jeannie? How are you feeling?" my aunt asked.

"As a matter of fact," I said, "very well. Is that why you called?"

"Yes." Her voice was bright and cheery. She sounded as if she were smiling. "Have a nice day." Click.

"What did she want?" my mother asked.

"I don't know. She said I should have a nice day." I put the receiver back.

"How come she didn't want me to have a nice day?" Richie asked.

"You're not named Jean," I said. "She only—holy smoke!" Holy blue smoke. Aunt Jean had asked Arthur if she could make a wish for somebody else.

She must have made a wish for me, and phoned to see if it was coming true.

"What is it?" my mother said. "You look as if you forgot to study for a test."

"Yes. No. Nothing." I jumped up from the table and ran to get my books. "I'm late. Bye."

"You're not late," my father said. "Why are you in such a hurry to get to school today?"

"Maybe she did study for a test," said Richie.

"Whatever," I said. "I feel dandy."

"That's what worries us." My mother laughed.

I was early. I was so early I had time to walk over to Lynn's house, even though it was six blocks out of the way. We usually met on Bayview Boulevard, which was halfway between our houses.

I couldn't wait to get to school. What kind of a wish had Aunt Jean made for me? Was it just that I be happy? That would be fine with me. That was the wish I should have made myself.

Or was it more specific? Would I be popular? Would Ned Bayer kiss me in real life?

Whatever wish she had made, I was sure it was coming true. There was no other explanation for this glorious day.

Lynn was just coming out of her house as I turned the corner onto Allegheny Avenue. I waved. "Hi!" I yelled.

We met in the middle of the block. She looked very surprised. Lynn wasn't used to seeing me cheerful either.

"Did you inherit a fortune?" she asked. "You look—I don't know. Radiant is the only word I can think of."

"That's a good word," I said. "That's the way I feel."

"But why?"

"It's a beautiful day, and a new beginning, and I—"

I wished I could tell her about Arthur and Aunt Jean, but she didn't remember about the lamp and she already thought I was acting weird.

"I decided to face life with a positive attitude," I said. "Today is the day I decided to start."

"That's great!" Lynn said.

"Do you have to know how to dance to join the dance club?" I asked.

"Most of the people are into ballet and modern dance," she said. "Why should you join a club you aren't interested in?"

"I think part of my new attitude should be a willingness to try new experiences and meet new people." I couldn't believe the words I heard coming out of my own mouth. I didn't sound like me at all. Aunt Jean and Arthur had certainly done a nifty job.

"I saw a notice on the bulletin board about joining the school magazine," Lynn said. "Why don't you try that? You were always good in English."

That was true. And I'd just written a book.

"I will," I said. "Thanks for telling me about it." I tried to sound casual. "Are Ned and Tiffany back together yet?"

"No," said Lynn. "I heard he totally dumped her."

I still couldn't understand why Ned was mad at Tiffany. Everything should have returned to normal when the wish was over.

Lynn smiled. "Totally," she repeated. "The coast is clear for you."

"Oh, come on," I said. "I was just curious about why they broke up."

"Sure. Just curious. That's why you blush and stammer every time you see him."

I blushed. "I d-d-do n-not."

Lynn laughed so hard she nearly dropped her books. "Of course you don't. The way I heard it is that Ned saw Tiffany at the movies with Barry Solomon when she thought Ned was going to be away for the weekend."

I nearly blurted out, "You mean it wasn't my fault?"

Ned and Tiffany's argument had nothing to do with my wishes. All along it had only been between them, and now Ned was free.

Just thinking about that made me blush.

I found myself saying "Hi" to every person I recognized in school that day. I'd never spoken to so many people in one day in my life.

It was easy. I said "Hi," they said "Hi." I smiled, they smiled. Some of them looked startled, but nobody ignored me.

Over and over I thought, "Thank you, Aunt Jean. I could never have done it without you."

I found the announcement about the school magazine on the first-floor bulletin board. The meeting was scheduled for today at three.

I was kind of disappointed that I didn't get a chance to see Ned now that I felt brave enough to talk to him. But there would be other days. I was sure Aunt Jean hadn't just wished for one day of happiness for me.

When the last bell rang I collected my books and my sweater and headed for room 322, where the magazine meeting was being held.

Suddenly I didn't feel so confident anymore. I was still a freshman, and probably a stranger to most of the people who were on the staff of the magazine.

This wasn't as simple as giving someone a casual greeting as I walked to my desk or my locker. But I thought of Aunt Jean, and I thought of Arthur, and I thought of Obi-Wan Kenobi saying, "May the Force be with you," and I walked into room 322.

And bumped straight into Ned Bayer, who was just inside the door.

I stood there, *on his foot,* blushing, panicking, and stammering. I was making a complete fool of myself. And I was still standing on his foot.

I took a deep breath. I removed my foot from his foot.

"Hi, Ned," I said.

"Well." He smiled. "At last. I was about to give up hope."

"You mean, nobody else wants t-to be on the m-magazine?"

"I wasn't talking about the magazine," he said. "I was talking about you."

"Me?"

"I thought you'd never say hello to me. Every time I look at you, you ignore me."

"You look at me?" I could hardly believe him.

"You didn't even notice me looking?" he asked.

"Oh, yes, I did—I mean, I didn't mean—"

"Hello," Ned said softly.

"Hello."

Seventeen

As eager as I had been to get to school that morning, I was almost as impatient to get home after the meeting. I headed straight for the phone and dialed Aunt Jean.

"You're incredible," I said the moment she answered. "You won't believe the things that happened to me today. *I* can hardly believe them."

I started reeling off the long list of reasons why I'd had a wonderful day.

"You're a great wisher," I said finally. "Thank you for the best day of my life."

"I didn't make a wish for you," she said.

"You did so. I know you did. That's why you called to find out how I felt this morning."

"I didn't, Jeannie," she said. "I called because I wanted you to *think* I made a wish for you."

"But you did! I never could have done all that stuff by myself."

I'd only been brave and self-confident because I thought I was touched with magic. I'd had Aunt Jean's wish working for me, and with it how could I fail?

How could she tell me that magic had nothing to do with it?

"I don't believe it," I said. "You're just telling me that to build up my self-esteem. So I'll think I did it all on my own. But I know I didn't."

"Yes you did," Aunt Jean insisted. "Hold on a minute."

"Hello?" said Arthur. "She didn't make a wish for you. That's the truth."

"That doesn't mean I won't make wishes for you," she said. "I'll probably make a lot of wishes. But this was sort of an experiment."

An experiment. Overnight I had become almost an entirely different person, and I was supposed to believe that wasn't magical?

"You let me know when there's anything you need," Aunt Jean said. "We'll take care of it."

"And listen," said Arthur. "Don't be a stranger. Come and visit once in a while."

I smiled. "Okey dokey," I said, and hung up the phone.

ABOUT THE AUTHOR

ELLEN CONFORD is the author of more than twenty books for children and young adults. She is a native New Yorker who now lives in Great Neck, New York, with her husband, David. She is a championship-level Scrabble® player, and also competes in crossword puzzle tournaments. Her popular novels for teenagers available in Bantam Starfire paperback editions are *Hail, Hail Camp Timberwood, Anything for a Friend,* and *The Things I Did for Love.*